3.1

Mail-Order Revenge

A novella

Angela K Couch

This is a work of fiction. Names, characters, businesses, places, events and incidents are either the products of the author's imagination or used in a fictitious manner. Any resemblance to actual persons, living or dead, or actual events is purely coincidental.

Copyright © 2016 Angela K Couch
Cover by Jessica Sprong – Design Junkie

All rights reserved. No part of this publication may be reproduced, distributed, or transmitted in any form or by any means, including photocopying, recording, or other electronic or mechanical methods, without the prior written permission of the author, except in the case of brief quotations embodied in critical reviews and certain other noncommercial uses permitted by copyright law. For permission requests, write to the author, addressed "Attention: Permissions Coordinator," at the address below.

angelakcouch@hotmail.com

Printed in the United States of America

Mail-Order Revenge/ Angela K Couch
    ISBN: 978-1530914739
    ISBN: 1530914736
    1. History—Romance.   2. Christian—Inspirational.   3.Mail-order Bride—Western

All scripture is taken from the KJV of the Bible

First Edition

14 13 12 11 10 / 10 9 8 7 6 5 4 3 2 1

To Corina and Kelly

Chapter 1

New York, 1882

It had to be him. Elizabeth Landvik's pulse sped as she read the advertisement yet again. Twenty-seven. Blue eyes. Blond hair. Tall. A description that could fit any number of men, but how many Axel Forsbergs were there in the territory of Arizona?

The sun made a steady retreat behind the row of buildings to the west, stretching shadows across the neat rows of ink marking the newspaper. Elizabeth rolled the paper and passed the boy a nickel. He usually let her read for free, but she wasn't ready to hand this one back to him.

Tightening her grip, she quickened her pace across the street to the boarding house where she shared a room with four other women who worked with her at the sewing factory. No wonder she'd found herself glancing over advertisements beseeching ladies to go west. This is what her life had been reduced to. Drudgery and cockroaches. And all because of the Forsbergs.

The stairs creaked and moaned as she vaulted up them. A piano's tink-tink followed her, souring her mood more. Laying her fingers across ivory keys and expressing herself in music had once been her passion, but her piano had been one of the first items sold from their estate.

Elizabeth slapped the door behind her and dropped onto her bed. A curse rang out from the other side of the small room where the newest addition, a woman in her late thirties, tried to sleep. "Have some respect, will you?" she snapped, pulling her pillow over her head.

Respect? Elizabeth ground her teeth as she turned away and smoothed the newspaper open beside her. Respect was a forgotten notion reserved for the upper and even middle-class. Perhaps she'd never been as grand as some of the ladies she saw riding by in their fine carriages, but she had once been a part of genteel society.

She pulled the pin from her hat and dropped both on the small chest containing all that remained of her worldly possessions—everything the auction and creditors hadn't stolen. Next she loosened the buttons of her jacket and slipped it off, her gaze never wandering from the paper. Why would an attractive and wealthy man like Axel Forsberg be so desperate for a bride as to write such an advertisement? No doubt there were more men than women that far west, but still...

Elizabeth didn't bother lighting a lamp. With the words memorized, there was no reason for it, and the last thing she needed was another tongue lashing. Heaven knew she'd had her fair share of those today at the factory.

She ran her fingers over her opposite palm, course and riddled with calluses. Broken nails. Aching wrists. Though nothing compared to the coals burning in her shoulders and back from hunching over bolts of fabric fourteen hours every day. To think, here she sat, forced to sew the same seam a hundred times a day, a thousand times a week, to sustain this meager existence, while somewhere to the west, the sun still hovered high in the sky over a huge ranch owned and run by Lars Forsberg and his son, built with the wealth they stole from her father.

She crumpled the newspaper and tossed it to the floor, then flopped onto her side. Elizabeth wiggled, working her body between the largest lumps in the mattress. The chill spring breeze leaking through the cracks around the window frame made her shiver, but she didn't bother reaching for her blanket. What was the point? It didn't compare to the block of ice residing in her center ever since Father lost his business and investments. They'd moved to that first drafty house where Mama succumbed to illness. And then Father, withering away before her eyes, drinking himself into an early grave.

They might as well have been murdered.

And soon Axel would be welcoming a bride to his prosperous ranch, giving Lars grandchildren to enjoy in his old age...

"How can I bear this?" Her words came with her breath. In truth, she couldn't bear it. Already the thought gnawed away at her resolve to stay sane.

Maybe that was her problem. Sanity. Logic. Neither had served her well. Maybe it was past time to put away reason and take matters into her own hands.

Elizabeth sat up so abruptly her vision momentarily darkened and her head began to throb. What if she answered the advertisement? If she could convince Mr. Forsberg that she was a good prospect for his wife, maybe there was a way to take back what they'd stolen. Maybe she could teach them what it felt like to have everything they loved snatched away.

Tomorrow she'd purchase stationary and make her reply. Father had never mixed home and business except for the annual Christmas party, but Axel had never turned his head her way and Lars had been too busy talking with their investors. Bedsides, she'd been a child then, not yet thirteen. Neither Forsberg was likely to recognize her now.

Spine stiff and jaw set, Elizabeth laid back down. She'd take her mother's maiden name and become the woman of Axel's dreams...and his nightmares.

Good thing she no longer believed in God or His judgment.

***

The three-year-old filly shifted as Axel settled his weight into the saddle. Every nerve seemed on fire with anticipation of what the next few seconds might bring. He deepened his breath and tried to relax his muscles. The horse continued to sidestep, turning a large circle. Axel eased the reins. Coming to a stop, the filly shook her head, and then her whole body as though with the hopes of dislodging the weight from her back.

With a click of his tongue, Axel encouraged her forward, a slight pressure applied to her ribs. Four steps. Then the animal's head dove between her legs. Axel grabbed for the tall iron horn and pressed his feet forward in the stirrups, all the while working with his free hand to pull the head up and to the left. The motion only gave a spin to the filly's attempt to throw him. Lurching in a tight circle like a rocking chair in a whirlwind, the filly bowed her back, not letting up until one of Axel's boots dislodged from the stirrup and he was forced into a premature dismount. On his backside.

A chuckle behind him made him cringe, but he pushed himself up and caught the horse before turning. "I thought you went to town."

Pa's eyes crinkled at the corners, but the mirth had left his face. "There and back again."

Axel's gut tightened, and he sent a prayer toward the heavens. Something wasn't being said. "Did you have another run-in with Harvey Cooper or one of the boys?"

Removing his hat, Pa wiped his wrist across his glistening brow. "No. I reckon they don't want trouble any more than we do."

"I hope so." With the Cooper's land bordering them on the west, there had already been terseness over water rights and a few stray heifers. The last thing they needed was a full out feud. But, if the Coopers were keeping to themselves, what had Pa looking like he'd committed a crime? "You got everything we needed?"

The older man raked his almost white hair back with his free hand and pressed his hat into place. He shook his head. "I couldn't be made to wait around. I'll go back tomorrow. I needed to show you this first." He fished a letter from his coat pocket and extended it over the fence.

It took Axel a couple attempts to take hold of the envelope as the filly nudged his arm with her nose, already bored with standing still. He narrowed his eyes, but not at the horse's antics. This wasn't the first envelope like this he'd seen, but usually Pa kept them to himself. Asking about the letters had fallen on deaf ears and usually turned the conversation to plans for the future, how many head of cattle they'd be running in five years, the benefit of starting with good bloodlines, and how nice it would be for Axel to have a son someday to inherit the results of their labor.

He eyed the words marking the front of the letter. "Who do we know in New York?" A stupid question considering his parents had emigrated there from Sweden before his birth, and it had been his home until nine years ago. That didn't change the fact that they had severed most every tie they'd had with that city after Mama's death.

"You'd best read the letter. Then come to the house, and we'll talk." Pa turned and walked away, his steps noticeably slower than usual.

The filly tried to nibble the paper as Axel drew it from the envelope. He released her reins and slipped through the planks of the corral. Leaning back into the raw wood, Axel stared at the delicate slant and flourish of the prettiest handwriting he'd seen since his mother's passing.

Dear Axel,

Thank you for agreeing to allow me to call you by your given name. I know we've never met, but it makes me feel as though we have. In a way, through our letters, I feel I know you better than any other person of my acquaintance. I look forward to finally joining you, and starting a life with you. I only have a few minutes to post this, but I wanted to inform you I have indeed received the funds you sent and have booked passage. By the time you receive this letter, I will be on my way to you. I should arrive by rail in Phoenix on the 27th of August. I am told there is a

stagecoach that can take me north from there.
Your devoted,
Eliza Danton

Axel's teeth began to hurt before he realized he was clenching his jaw...and the paper. He glanced back at the filly. He really should finish with her now—save his good saddle from her attempts at pushing it off by rolling over—but his anger wouldn't do the horse any favors. He'd be back.

Lengthening his stride, only minutes saw him at the door to the cabin he and Pa built when they'd first arrived over three years ago. Of course, they'd only started with the main room and added the two smaller ones later. He shoved the door open and strode across the floor, before slamming the paper to the table. Pa reclined in his chair, apparently unaffected.

"Who is this woman, why is she writing to me like we know each other, and what in the world is she coming here for?" Not much breath remained in his lungs, but Axel blew it out anyway.

Pa's lined face twitched a smile. "Did you think I'd let you hide up here and grow old alone?"

"Obviously I'm not alone." Axel folded his arms across his chest. "I wouldn't have to worry about your insane schemes if I were."

"Sending for a woman from the East is hardly insane or unheard of. I told you if you didn't start going to Phoenix or Prescott to find yourself a wife, I'd take matters into my own hands." Pa's arms crossed to match Axel's. "Maybe next time you'll heed me a little better."

A next time? If his father had anything to do with it, he'd be stuck with a wife and passel of young'uns before he could bat an eye. From the sounds of it, the wife was already on the way. Anger flared. "You could have at least said something to me before dragging some poor soul across the country for no reason."

"Why? So you can put up a fuss like you are now, and drag your heels like you've been doing since you learned to walk? The woman is on her way, and you will not disappoint her."

Axel threw up his hands. There was never any reasoning with the old man. "But I don't even know her. You're the one who's been corresponding with the woman." Now Axel quirked a smile. "You marry her."

Pa only shook his head. "I've already experienced what a good woman brings to a man's life. Your mother and my memories of her are all I'll ever need. That's what I want you to have, but you're too focused on this land and those cows. You'd rather get dropped on your backside in manure than go into town and talk to a woman. So here you have it, my gift to you. I've prayed long and hard about this woman, and I feel she'll be just what you need."

Prayer. How could he argue with that? Pa had never led him wrong before.

Axel sighed and sank defeated into the nearest chair. A neat stack of envelopes caught his eye, piled not far from where the last one had fallen. He dragged them to him and opened the one on top. It only took a few minutes to read all the letters. A Christian woman who worked hard to support herself since she had no family to speak of. Maybe Pa was right. He could provide a better life for her than that stuffy old city.

And it would save a heap of time and hassle trying to find and woo a woman. He could only pray she looked as good, and was as honorable, as paper and ink suggested.

Chapter 2

The town of Bumble Bee appeared to consist of the sign bearing its peculiar name and a cluster of rustic buildings. Every muscle ached, but there was no relief when the stage lurched to a stop. Could this really be her destination? Thankfully her stay would be short in this wilderness. Elizabeth wouldn't linger a day longer than it took to wreak some havoc and find what rightfully belonged to her family.

Only one other passenger had taken the stage from the station at Phoenix, and he had ridden up with the driver who appeared more concerned with the horses than helping her out. It was left to Elizabeth to find the latch on the stagecoach door and shove it open. Her legs, numb from being jostled and jolted most of two days, faltered on the two small steps, and she hurried to jump to the rutted ground. For a moment the earth felt as though it shifted. She steadied herself on one of the large wheels.

Hallelujah, she'd finally arrived. Elizabeth glanced down at the once brilliant navy blue jacket she wore over her cream dress, both bought new with a little money remaining from what Forsberg had sent her. Now the jacket appeared a smoky brown, coated generously with Arizona dust. She shook her skirts, but only succeeded in making herself sneeze.

Nothing for her cleanliness until she found a washbasin, Elizabeth straightened her hat and raised her gaze to the twig of a town called Bumble Bee. US Calvary station. Saloon. Livery. And a man leaning against the box of a wagon, watching her. Her stomach clenched. Even at this distance, and after so many years, she recognized the unruly gold locks and somber smile of Axel Forsberg.

He seemed to heave a breath before pushing away from the wagon and starting toward her. Elizabeth had thought him grown when she'd seen him in the east, but he looked so much taller than she remembered. Broader, too. She rotated away and reached up for the chest she'd kept on the seat beside her.

She'd been mad thinking she could pull off this deceit. What if he did recognize her? He'd no doubt leave her stranded without more than a dollar in her reticule. She might make it as far as Prescott. But then what? What sort of employment was available for a woman in this barren wasteland?

She glanced sideways at the Bumble Bee saloon and shuddered. Not just because of the predicament she'd landed herself in, but who named a town after an insect? She had no choice but follow through with her plan and hope she had indeed matured beyond recognition.

"Let me get that for you, Miss." The deep rumble of Axel's voice at her side hitched the breath into her throat. "You're Miss Danton, I assume?"

His arm brushed hers as he reached for the chest, and she scooted aside. "Yes." Elizabeth forced herself to look at him and curve her lips in an upward direction. Goodness, his eyes were even bluer than she remembered them. "And you are Mr. Forsberg." The flirtatious tone she'd managed with ink on stationery completely escaped her now. She'd hated him and his father for so long, how would she ever pull off this performance? Elizabeth steeled herself, ignoring the heat rising within her.

He nodded, his gaze growing appreciative and far too intrusive. "But like agreed to in the letters, Axel is fine... Eliza." He glanced down at the chest and then inclined his head toward the wagon. "I'll load this, and then come back for the rest of your luggage. After that, we should talk."

Elizabeth started nodding, then shook her head. "Um...everything I brought with me is in that chest. But, yes, I suppose there are things we need to discuss." She brushed past him, anything to remove herself from his steady gaze, though she sensed it followed her, as did he. She crossed the street and took hold of the wagon to steady herself.

Axel hefted the chest over the side into the back and cleared his throat. "Eliza, it means a lot to me that you were willing to come all the way out here, thousands of miles from home, to marry a man you've never met, but before we go any further, there is something you need to know." His tone suggested apology. But what would he have to apologize for unless he planned to send her back? All that way?

"What would that be?"

He scratched the chopped curls at the nape of his neck. "Honesty and keeping one's word is bedrock to me, and I won't let this marriage be built upon lies."

Elizabeth felt the blood rush from her head. She should have known he'd see past her charade.

"I didn't write you those letters."

"What? Pardon me?" The muscles in her jaw slackened from both relief and surprise. "Then who—"

"My father."

"Your—"

"He thought I needed some prodding because I've never made much effort courting. None really. The ranch is important to me. I actually grew up in New York too, but it was never the life for me. So I convinced my Pa we should come west. I've spent over five years working for others, learning the ropes, and the last three years have been sunk into making a go of this ranch." He gave a chuckle and a shake of his head. "What I mean to say is, I haven't had the time for finding myself a wife, but that doesn't mean I don't want one. I've read your letters, and Pa probably did a well enough job portraying me in the ones he wrote. We're more alike than I often care to admit, but there it is. I'll keep his word and marry you, if that's what you still want."

The thought that she had been writing Lars Forsberg and not Axel the past few months seared her chest. At least Axel was the less guilty of the two. And now he stood here asking her what she wanted. She had answers enough. To not marry him. To have her parents alive.

To go home to the life she'd enjoyed as a child.

But there was no going back.

Axel ducked his head and rubbed a knuckle against his temple as a smile tugged at his mouth. "Truth is, Eliza, I wasn't so sure about this whole arrangement, but after seeing you, I think I might be coming around. And not just because you're as pretty as you are. When I saw you climbing down from that stage, it occurred to me the kind of courage it must have taken for a woman like you to travel all this way on your own. And I respect that. I don't think marrying you is a decision I'm going to regret."

Elizabeth's face warmed. Not from his praise, but from the fact that making him regret this marriage was foremost on her mind.

"Do you need time to think about it?"

"No." She squared her shoulders, the verse in the Bible about not looking back after setting a hand to the plow coming to mind. Strange. She hadn't read the book since Mama's death. "I agreed to marry you, and I shall."

***

Axel couldn't help but raise a brow to Eliza Danton's confident answer, because he'd honestly expected the dark-haired beauty to breathe a sigh of relief and hurry back to the stagecoach. He couldn't miss the rigidness of her spine, or the narrowing of her gaze when she'd first looked across the street at him. Was he not what she expected? Or was she simply exhausted from her journey and wished to have this ordeal over with.

Ordeal. For some reason that wasn't a word he'd associated with his own wedding. But understandably the woman—Eliza—just wanted a nice comfortable place to rest and recover from thousands of miles of track and trail. The strangest thing was the calm he'd felt upon finally seeing her. And not just because she was pretty. Nope. There was something about her, a familiarity. He could only assume it was the good Lord's way of letting him know Eliza was right for him.

Axel reached past her to grab his hat from the seat. He shoved it onto his head. "Then we'd best hurry."

"Hurry?"

He waved his hand to the stagecoach. "We don't have our own preacher here, but Pastor Hartley has been in town for the past two weeks and leaves on today's stage. In another half hour the horses will be changed and Sam, the driver, will have had his dinner and be ready to go on to Prescott."

Eliza's cheeks lost an ounce of their color,

and her hand pressed to her stomach as she glanced from the stage to the wagon and then to him. She raised her pretty chin. "If we must." Her tone carried a barb, and her dark eyes turned hard. Perhaps he'd spoken too fast about no regrets.

"Whether the preacher was leaving today or not, wouldn't have made much difference. As you can see, there isn't anywhere suitable for a single woman to stay here in town, and it wouldn't be proper for you to come out to the ranch unchaperoned."

Her shoulders slumped. "Of course."

Axel took two steps toward the station where the pastor waited, and then turned back. She hadn't moved. Was the reality of this situation so much worse than she had imagined? Or was it the realization that she was marrying a complete stranger? He had just admitted to not writing those letters.

"Is there anything you would like to know about me before we proceed?"

She met his gaze but said nothing.

"I'm not given to drink or losing my temper, though I admit to having one. I'll work hard to make sure you never want for anything, and I put my faith in the Good Lord." His smile came easier as he thought of the words in her letters of devotion to God and her love of the

Bible. "I'm glad we'll have that to share."

Axel extended his arm, and she took it. Nothing else was said as he led her across the street and into the station office where the pastor sat with his luggage. The older man stood as they approached, and straightened his black suit.

"Good, good, she did make it in time. I'm so glad, but with how fast Sam is shoveling food into his mouth," he motioned to where the driver sat with a plate of beans at a small table on the opposite side of the room, "I suggest we hurry." The pastor gave a wink and stepped around his suitcase.

Axel removed his hat. He wasn't sure it was necessary, but it seemed the thing to do. He tapped the brim against his leg as the pastor quoted a short verse from Genesis about leaving parents and cleaving to one's wife, and then began with the vows. Axel gave a ready yes. He'd already promised as much. Eliza answered as quick.

"Before God and this witness," the pastor again waved to Sam, who nodded, "I declare you husband and wife. You may kiss your bride, Mr. Forsberg."

Axel looked to Eliza, who stood resolute, not an expression on her face and not looking at anything in particular. As much as her full lips beckoned, it wouldn't be right to take advantage of their marriage until she was ready and willing.

***

Elizabeth pressed her eyes closed as the warmth of Axel's mouth brushed her cheek, his nearness smothering. He squeezed her shoulder as he drew away, and then turned to the parson to thank him. A few minutes later, he led her back to the wagon and helped her up onto the seat.

It was done. She was now his wife. As a young girl, she may have dreamed of such, but now it was nothing more than the price of her retribution.

Chapter 3

"Bumble Bee seems rather sparse." One of the wheels dropped over a rut, and Elizabeth gripped the edge of the wagon seat to keep from being thrown. Even the stagecoach had been smoother than this.

"Yep." Axel seemed unaffected by the rough terrain as they traveled higher into the mountains. "You have to ride down to Phoenix, or on to Prescott, if you want anything but the basics. I often just order what I need and they bring it on the stage, or with freight wagons."

"But what about everything else?" She tried to keep her voice casual. "Like a bank?"

"Do you need one?"

"Me? No...I... Not right now, anyways. I just wondered."

"We haven't needed to bother with one yet. Paid cash money for everything."

Of course they had. Elizabeth tipped her head away so he wouldn't be able to read her thoughts. "You said you grew up in New York, as well."

She glanced over to see his nod.

"May I ask why you left?" The second question Elizabeth had been rehearsing in her mind the past couple of hours while lurching with the wagon along the side of a mountain. Father had never given all the details of Lars Forsberg's betrayal, or how he'd destroyed the business they had built together and stolen their profits.

Axel looked at her and smiled. After her initial silence, he was probably relieved that she still had a voice. "I'd always been a little restless, but after my mother passed, I didn't feel anything really held me in the city, or in the East, for that matter. When I told my father I wanted to go west, he decided he could use the change—Mama dying was difficult for him."

Elizabeth shifted on the hard bench, ready for the last leg of her journey to be over. Especially now that she could place more of the blame on Axel. He'd encouraged his father to break with hers. For all she knew, it had also been his idea to cheat her father. "You—I mean, your father—wrote that you have cattle and quite a few horses. It must have taken a lot of hard work and a significant investment to build a ranch up here?"

"It wasn't easy or cheap." He snapped the reins over the horses' backs to encourage them across a shallow, but rocky stream. A glistening spray from the wheels drew her attention, and she tried to pull the hem of her skirt farther out of the way—the pale fabric not at all suited to this wilderness. She had to give up the attempt as it was all she could do to remain seated. Axel's arm stole around her waist, steadying her. Elizabeth fought the urge to swat him away, which would do nothing for her plight to stay on board.

She waited until the trail smoothed a little, and he withdrew his arm, before putting forth her next question. "Did you earn enough working as a ranch hand those five years you mentioned, or did you come west with what you needed?"

"The wages I earned were almost enough for the cattle and supplies we needed, so we were able to put some of what we brought with us away for hard years. It pays to be prepared."

Which meant most of her family's wealth was probably intact, and since they'd had no use for banks, the money was likely hidden out at the ranch somewhere. She would find it. "How much farther?"

"Not long now." Axel nodded to the meadow on the right. "All this is Forsberg land east of this trail."

"And west?" The grass was just as green on that side.

"Harvey Cooper owns that. If you take the trail that broke off just before the stream, it'll lead you up to their place. They're our closest neighbors, and we try to keep things peaceful as that water feeds most of our ranch and it flows through their land first."

Elizabeth settled into the seat, only to wince as her tailbone met the unforgiving surface. She'd probably bruised it crossing the stream. Thankfully a cabin appeared not far ahead, flanked with a barn and corrals.

"Here we are. This valley was nothing but wild grass and evergreens a few years ago. Now it's home." Axel looked at her, his blue eyes almost as bright as the clear sky overhead, but with the haze of smoke toward the centers, like the wisp rising from the cabin's stone chimney. "I hope you come to love it here as much as I do."

Elizabeth returned his smile. She'd play the part until she found that money. As the wagon eased to a stop just outside the cabin, she breathed a sigh and slid to the edge of the seat. The air caught in her throat as the front door swung open and Lars Forsberg bounded out, taking the two small steps in one swift stride.

Axel was on his way around the wagon to help her down, but Lars beat him. "Welcome, welcome!"

Elizabeth lost control of her muscles for a moment—her thoughts too. This was the man who had destroyed her life. Thank goodness he had no idea who she was or the devastation she planned to leave behind. She was still stationary when his hands found her waist and lifted her down. His blue eyes, so much like Axel's, looked all too pleased as he stood her on her feet.

"Eliza, I can't say how happy I am that you're here. Come inside. Axel will bring your luggage."

"Pa..." Axel hurried to his father's side, but his gaze found Elizabeth's and lingered. He slowed. "I'll come back for your things." His eyes grew thoughtful. "My mother would be disappointed in me if I didn't start this marriage properly."

Before Elizabeth could guess what he meant, Axel swept her into his arms. A yelp escaped her as she grabbed for his neck. Mostly it was a reflex to steady herself, but the urge to strangle him also came to mind...but was quickly dismissed if only for the fact he would drop her if she did.

Once past the threshold, Axel released her

to the floor, the hint of a smile making him appear all too roguish. She turned away and smoothed her skirts. The large room held a table, chairs, and a monster cast-iron stove. She couldn't fathom how they'd gotten it through the mountains, never mind into the cabin. Unless they had built their home around it. Warmth radiated from the stove, filling the room with the aroma of seared beef. Her stomach pinched. She hadn't considered eating anything tonight, but suddenly hunger gnawed.

Lars hurried past her, plucking the lid from the frying pan so the heavenly smell flooded her and made her mouth water. He flipped the thick slabs of sizzling meat. "Let me get these on the table for you. They're about done. Go sit yourself down and rest."

Elizabeth was incapable of declining. She sank into the nearest chair, not much more on her mind than food as he forked three large steaks onto a plate. From the oven he pulled a handful of potatoes with their skins still on. Axel laid out forks and knives, and a jar of butter. Then fixed her a plate.

"Both Pa and I quite enjoy cooking, so hopefully, it won't take too long to put something on those bones of yours."

Elizabeth's face heated, but she did her best not to react. He was right. She was much too skinny, and often ailed from not eating enough. That would change once she found her family's money.

She took up the knife and fork when Lars cleared his throat. "Dear Lord, we thank Thee for this food and all the plenty Thou has blessed us with. We especially thank Thee at this time for Eliza. We pray she comes to feel at home in our valley, and that Thou wilt bless their marriage. Amen."

Elizabeth's grip tightened on the knife as she impaled the steak with her fork. God-praising hypocrites were the worst kind.

Not much was said while they ate their dinner, but Elizabeth finished first and pushed to her feet. "I am afraid I'm not feeling well. And very exhausted."

"Of course." Axel hurried around the table to her. "I'll show you to our room and then get your luggage."

Our room. His words sank to her stomach and fermented there. She glanced to her empty plate and the knife laying across it. Then sat back down. "I'll wait while you get my things."

As he turned away, she glanced to Lars, whose gaze followed his son. She slipped the knife from her plate and into the folds of her skirt.

***

Axel glanced from the bed, to his new wife, and back again. The mattress looked narrower than it did this morning. Not that he minded much, but he got the feeling she did. She stared at the bed, her face colorless, her hands wrapped in the fabric of her dress. She probably wasn't admiring the quilt with its intricate patchwork design.

"My mother sewed the quilt," he said with hopes of easing the tension in the room. "A wedding present."

Eliza's head came up. "I don't understand. You said your mother…"

"She made it when she first got sick. She was in bed for several months before the Lord took her. Knowing that she wouldn't live long enough to see me married, she gave it to me to put away until the day came." Axel took the corner of the quilt and folded it down. "For now. It's been tucked away in a trunk until yesterday when I pulled it out to air. Never used it yet."

Something softened in him, and he looked to his bride. Strange to think they had only met that morning and now they were husband and wife. "You don't look well. Come, lie down."

One of her hands rose to her stomach. "I do

feel quite unwell. Perhaps it would be best if you slept elsewhere tonight. Suppose I'm ill and you were to catch it."

"Most likely you're only tired. A good night's sleep will set you right." By the looks of her she'd probably be too nervous to sleep with him at her side. "But I'll take my pillow and a blanket out tonight in case you're right."

She remained silent, not even uttering a thank you as Axel took what he needed and left. He closed the door behind him and shot his father a glare. Pa leaned back in his chair, arms folded, but looking not at all surprised that his son had been evicted from his own bed. Instead he appeared amused.

"How was the wedding?"

Axel replied with a grunt as he dropped the pillow and blanket on the floor near the fireplace and crossed back to the table. "Well enough. It's the marriage that has me concerned."

"Give Eliza some time. I doubt she's had an easy life. And I'm sure it was difficult for her to come all this way. Time will let her get to know you and cure what's ailing her."

Axel rested his hands on the back of a chair, but uncertainty and restlessness continued to build in him. He pushed away. "I'm going to go ride out to the south pasture and check on those heifers. Don't wait up for me."

Chapter 4

Elizabeth smothered out the crowing of a rooster with her pillow—its scent woodsy. Like Axel. Her head bumped the handle of the knife she'd stashed there last night, and she moaned, shifting away from it and pulling the pillow off her face. Morning lit the room with brilliant rays through the small window, revealing a cascade of minuscule dust motes. Dropping the pillow onto the empty side of the bed, Elizabeth pulled the quilt under her chin and listened. She felt naked in just her nightgown. What if Axel needed a change of clothes or something else from his room?

Their room.

She shuddered.

The cabin sat in silence, so she got up and pulled on the dress she'd worn yesterday. With days of endless travel, her first act of business would be to find a wash tub and clean her clothes.

Her plan changed as soon as she stepped into the main room of the cabin. Completely abandoned, a folded stack of bedding testifying that Axel, and probably Lars as well, were up and busy with their day. The sooner she found the money, the sooner she could leave—something she needed to do before Axel decided he wanted theirs to be a real marriage. She thought of the knife. As much as she wanted him to suffer for his part in her family's distress, she didn't want to see him dead. And definitely not at her hand.

Elizabeth began her search in the main room, checking for any sort of hiding places along the walls, loose rocks in the fireplace, and then through each tin box of foodstuffs. Flour, ground oats, coffee, and even matches, but no money. She moved to the second bedroom where Lars slept. Not much in there besides a tall-backed chair beside the bed, and a large wooden chest against the wall. What might it contain? The hinges creaked as she opened the lid, joining the song of the hinges on the front door of the cabin. She dropped the chest lid and scampered out of the room.

Axel plopped his hat to the table and raised one of his honey-colored eyebrows. "Were you looking for something?"

Attempting to regulate her breath and

pulse, Elizabeth gave a nod. "I was... I need...a...wash basin. For my clothes."

"Oh. Of course. It's hanging outside." Axel's words died long before his stare. After a minute, he cleared his throat and moved to the stove. Crouching, he opened one of the lower compartments and shoved another log into the heart of the dying fire. "After I fix some breakfast, I'll fetch you the tub and fill it."

Elizabeth wiped her moist palms down her skirts as she inched closer. "I'm sure you have other things you need to do. If you show me where everything is, I can manage." Not that breakfast was at all on her mind. Curiosity about the contents of that chest overrode her hunger.

"Nonsense. Anything else can hold. Besides, with how busy life usually is up here, breakfast might be the only honeymoon we have." He cracked a smile then plucked a large jar of doughy mixture from one of the middle shelves and spooned a generous dollop into a wooden bowl. "And trust me, this is the best sourdough west of the Mississippi river. Add a little more flour and some eggs, and I'll cook you up some of the fluffiest flapjacks you've ever enjoyed."

Since he wasn't going anywhere, Elizabeth seated herself and settled in to watch Axel cradle the bowl in one arm as he added ingredients and stirred with the other. A memory surfaced of the large dining room in her childhood home, entering with Mother for the only dinner they had shared with Father's partner and his family. She had a very faint picture of what Mrs. Forsberg had looked like, because Elizabeth had been much too focused on the son, almost a man and one of the handsomest in her young opinion. He'd stood as she'd found her seat and she'd felt so much like a woman. But no doubt he had seen her just as she was—a child. Still, she'd waited impatiently for the next Christmas party—one that had never been held—and dreamt of the day she'd be old enough to draw his attention.

She cleared away the memory with a cough. "I never considered you the domestic sort."

"Though, you have known me for less than a day." He winked. "I imagine it will take some time to fully become acquainted."

Elizabeth's body heated as her thoughts read deeper into his words than hopefully he'd intended. One thing was for sure, by the way he looked at her, she now had Axel Forsberg's full attention. And she could use that to her advantage if she had the mind. What better way for him to feel the pain they had caused her than by letting him fall in love, and then breaking his heart.

A smile came easily to her face.

***

Axel struggled to return his attention to the batter. The way Eliza's smile lit up her face did something strange to his insides. He'd do about anything to keep that smile on her lips.

"I was thinking last night that maybe come winter, when I have a little more time, I'll start felling more trees, build a second cabin."

The smile was replaced by an inquisitive pout. "A second cabin?"

Axel turned to the stove for his favorite skillet and knifed in some butter. "I noticed your face when you saw Pa and realized he'd be living with us. And I can't blame you for wanting a place of our own. I talked with him this morning and he agreed with me. In fact, he suggests we build a smaller cabin for him and we stay here where we'll have room for children when they come."

A choking cough brought his head around. Eliza held one hand over her mouth while the other fanned her face.

"Are you all right?"

"Of course. Fine." Her smile returned, but

with a hint of mischievousness to it. Just as attractive. "Let's not hurry, though. Like you said, we've known each other less than a day."

"It'll be winter before I have time to start on the cabin."

"I wasn't talking about the cabin."

"Then what?"

Rosiness blossomed in her cheeks. "Children."

As Axel turned back to the stove, the warmth of the fire touched his face. She probably eluded to what came before children—something that had lingered in his mind last night as he'd tried to get comfortable on the floor. Axel quickly spooned some of the batter into the skillet before the butter burned. This was an easier topic to breach while faced away from her. "I'll leave the timing to you." Though he was beginning to hope she didn't take too long.

"Thank you."

When the first pancake was cooked to perfection, Axel flipped it onto a plate and set it before Eliza, already decked with a generous amount of butter and the prickly pear jelly he'd made himself that summer. He set the skillet off the heat so he could watch her first bite. Pleasure stretched across her face, as it probably did his.

He pulled the coffee pot back over the heat, and returned to cooking while she ate. As soon as her fork clanked to the plate he offered her more. And she took it—good woman. He wouldn't have his wife blown away by the next decent wind that swept over the mountains.

"Where did you learn to cook so well?" Eliza waved off a third helping.

"When we first came west, Pa got us a job handling a chuck wagon on a cattle drive. We hadn't much experience before that, but it was what work was available." Axel dumped in the last of the doughy batter then turned to her and rested his forearms against the back of a chair, leaning forward. "They had this bible of a cookbook, so we tried our hands at something 'til it tasted right, then moved on to the next recipe. We'd compete to see whose food would get eaten first by the cowpokes. Real fun." He chuckled at the memory and shook his head, grateful that his wife didn't seem the type that would kick him away from the stove, telling him it wasn't his place. "For a while we tossed around the idea of opening an eating house of sorts, but that would mean living in a larger town, and I like it up here."

Eliza pushed a bitty crumb around her plate and through a puddle of melted butter. "And so you hauled that monstrosity of a stove up here so you could cook to your heart's content."

"That's the fact of it." Axel relaxed, liking the way loose strands of rich brown hair fell beside her oval face. The odor of a charring flapjack assaulted his nose. He spun to rescue his breakfast, but he'd swallow down burnt food any day if it meant he'd get to keep this pretty distraction. Pa was right. He just needed to give Eliza some time.

***

After her clothes were washed and hung—thankfully the line was behind the cabin so her undergarments weren't on display for the men—Elizabeth wandered out to the barn and corrals. She'd familiarize herself with options for leaving when the time came.

Horses. There were two of the creatures nibbling on the summer grass in a small pasture just to the right of the barn, and three more in a corral to the left. She made her way in that direction and mounted the bottom plank of the fence so she could see beyond. In a round arena, the ground beat to powder, Axel perched on top a muscular animal the color of caramel. She squinted to try to make out what he was doing, but from the looks of it, nothing.

He just sat there, shoulders slumped, complete focus on the horse under him.

Curious, she worked her way around the first corral, and then quickened her pace to where Lars stood watching. Neither man looked her direction, but the horse did. Its ears perked high and its eyes widened. In an instant the horse reared and spun, then dove its nose to the ground and began to buck. Axel remained seated for all of seven seconds before tumbling heels-over-head and flat on his back. She winced at the thud. Then darted forward to see if he'd survived.

"Are you all right?"

A long moan was the only answer he gave as he rolled into his side, and then pushed himself up. He paused halfway to brace his hands on his knees and try for a breath. When he did straighten, his hand stole up to massage his temples. He groaned. "I'm alive."

She covered a smirk behind her hand. "I was going to ask if you could teach me to ride, but after that, I think I'd prefer to learn how to hitch the wagon."

Stretching his back, Axel moved to catch his horse. He secured one of the reins and came to the nearest fence. "This lady is just a little stubborn about things like saddles. Don't worry, I have the mount for you. That little gray mare in that next corral will do your beck and call with a smile on her face."

Elizabeth met Axel's gaze and placed a smile on her own face. "Really? I don't think I've ever seen a horse that looked pleased."

"Oh, the ones around here are quite happy critters." He gave his horse a firm rub on the neck, and then led her toward the center of the pen. "If you'd been listening, I'm sure you would have heard Desert Lady here chuckling to herself a few minutes ago." Axel eyed the stirrup, and then looked back to Elizabeth. "It might be better if I come find you when I'm finished here."

Elizabeth retreated. He probably didn't want her startling the horse again. "Only because I'm not quite ready to become a widow." Watching him break his neck wasn't part of her plan. It would only save him from what she did have in store.

Chapter 5

Axel dragged the saddle from the little mare's back and set it aside as his wife took up a brush and began currying the gray coat, almost black in places with sweat. "You're a good rider. I was worried when you first got astride, but not for long."

Eliza worked the bristles over the animal's hip, a subtle smile giving added form to her mouth. "I have ridden before and received training. It's just been a few years, and I'm not used to such a cumbersome saddle."

A chuckle rumbled from his chest. "Well, the mare is yours now, and you can ride her whenever you like. You can rename her, too."

Smoothing the brush over the silken coat, Eliza worked her way to the animal's face, her expression studious and her lips pursed. "What about Stitches."

"Stitches?" Not at all what Axel imagined she'd choose.

The smile slipped from Eliza's face. "I slaved away in that sewing factory for over four years, and I won't go back. I won't forget why I came here."

Axel stepped behind her and braced her shoulders, wishing he could remove the burden that seemed to remain over them. But all he could do was let her know that he was there for her now and she would never have to go back to that life.

Eliza twisted away and dropped the brush to the ground. "I'm tired. I think I'll retire early tonight." She scuttled from the barn and hurried toward the house.

Blowing out his breath, Axel stooped for the brush and finished with the mare. Then he led her back to the pasture. A full hour passed before the chores were complete. He washed off at the well and made his way to the cabin. Pa sat alone, dinner already on the table. One plate showed the residue of stew. Good. Eliza had eaten. Axel only downed a few spoonfuls before he pushed away from the table and collected his pillow and blanket from the floor.

"Thanks, Pa. I'm done in. I'll see you in the morning."

"G' night, son."

The bedroom was dim with the setting sun stealing away beyond the mountain, but enough light remained to make out Eliza's form tucked under his mother's quilt, eyes watching him. Axel tossed the pillow onto his side of the bed and then perched on the end to pull off his boots and socks. He unbuttoned his shirt. What would Mama think of his new bride? He wasn't aware of a person she hadn't liked. She'd been the epitome of charity and gentleness…especially to her son and husband.

Down to his long underwear, Axel slipped under the quilt next to Eliza. She rolled to face away from him, so he settled onto his back and stared up at the rough-hewn rafters above as they sank into shadow. He relaxed his muscles, letting the pain of the day seep from them. Desert Lady had thrown him once more before she settled and let him ride her. Thankfully tomorrow was the Sabbath and the Lord had declared it a day of rest. His body needed one. It would also give him more time with Eliza—something he looked forward to.

He turned onto his side to see his wife. Her dark hair lay in waves across the pillow, filling the space between them. Axel couldn't resist touching the ends, feeling the silkiness at the tips of his fingers. Maybe someday soon she'd let him sink his hands into her tresses and pull her close. Just to hold. The sweet fragrance, like his mother's summer flower bed, filled his lungs, and he deepened his breath.

"Goodnight, Eliza."

"Goodnight."

Axel let a lock of her hair slip between his thumb and forefinger. Mama's hair was brown too, but not this dark, and she always wore it piled on the back of her head, or in a thick braid when she'd been confined to her bed. She'd lain there for weeks, propped up with pillows so she could stitch the dainty roses into the array of colored fabric for this quilt.

"Why is this so important to you, Mama?" he'd asked her a few days before she slipped into the eternities. Her hands shook, making each stitch an exercise of will.

"Mostly selfish reasons," she'd said, her smile brightening her eyes as it always did. "I want to leave a mark upon your life. Just you remember, Axel, nothing will make you more miserable, or bring you more joy, than the woman you someday marry. Marriage is like a quilt. It's patching two lives together, with children to follow. You can tack the cloth together and pray it holds enough to keep you warm, or you can create a work of art that will add color and beauty to your life as well as protect you from the cold."

Axel ran his hand over the quilt, her final words resonating within him.

"Make something beautiful."

***

Eliza's heart sped as Axel's fingers wrapped over her arm. Her hand slipped under her pillow to find the hilt of the knife. He'd promised to let her decide when they would consummate their marriage, but she also knew he couldn't be believed. Her father had once trusted this family and they had driven him and Mother into an early grave.

"Eliza?"

"What?" She struggled to swallow.

"I want this to be a real marriage. I know it'll take time, but I promise to give you my whole heart. I want to be a good husband to you." He paused and the warmth of his breath seeped through her hair as he drew nearer. He laid a kiss just above her ear. "Help me."

The room fell silent so all she could hear was the thudding in her chest. And his. After a moment he withdrew. The mattress shifted as he rolled away. Still his warmth and presence filled the bed, making her feel overheated even in the linen nightgown. She released the knife but didn't move until the last of the light faded and his breathing deepened with sleep. If Axel and his father thought they could take what they wanted, and then build a perfect life for themselves without any consequences, they'd soon discover how mistaken that notion was.

Minutes extended as darkness filled the room and silence fell over the cabin. Only a slight glow through the window suggested a part moon. When she was certain everyone slept, and she couldn't stand the wait any longer, Elizabeth slipped from the bed and pulled on her shawl. Feet bare, she tiptoed to the end of the bed and picked Axel's boots from the floor. She didn't put them on until she was outside. Then plodded toward the corrals. Desert Lady raised her head as Elizabeth approached. A beautiful horse. No wonder Axel considered her worth the effort.

As Elizabeth took hold of the rope fastening the gate closed, memories of her father returned with potency. The day he had come home and collapsed at the table with a sob. "We are ruined. Forsberg has destroyed us. He's left us with nothing. There's no money left. The business, the house, everything. It's lost."

He'd sat there, weeping like a child. She'd never seen Father cry before. And nothing had ever scared her more.

Elizabeth swung the gate wide, and then started back to the cabin.

***

Axel felt no hurry to climb out of bed the next morning, not with his pretty wife lying beside him, her eyes closed, the usual tension in her body gone. She'd tossed a little during the night, bruising his shoulder with her elbow, and now faced him, fast asleep. Tucking his arm under his head, he watched her. He'd have to talk to Pa about Mama's wedding ring—he should have thought of it sooner. She'd wanted Axel to pass it to his wife.

The thought made him smile. *His wife.*

What sort of life would they build together? After seeing her up to her elbows in sudsy water yesterday, and later, how she'd taken to riding, it was easy to picture working side by side as they grew old together. His thinking might be premature after only two days of acquaintance, but there was something about her...like he'd met her before.

Axel dismissed the thought. He would have remembered those full lips and large olive-shaped eyes. Though, how old would she have been when he left New York? Almost ten years ago?

Pounding on the door halted his calculations. Axel rotated and sprung from the bed, grabbing for his pants.

Pa's voice filtered through the solid wood. "Lady got out somehow and has gone missing. Best hurry and get your boots on."

Axel grabbed them from where he'd dropped them last night and charged the door.

"What is it? What's happened?" Eliza sat up in bed, keeping the quilt to her throat. Her tousled hair hung about her shoulders. Even groggy and with red marks on her face showing the creases of the pillow case, she was beautiful.

He paused and shoved his foot into one of the boots. "Desert Lady's gone."

"Your horse?"

He gave a nod, while switching to hop on the other foot to pull the second boot on. "I'll have to go after her. Hopefully she hasn't gone too far." Dragging his gaze from Eliza, he groaned, his muscles even stiffer than before he'd gone to bed. So much for a restful day.

Pa was already at the corral in question by the time Axel blinked the morning sun from his eyes. He pulled his Stetson low.

"She must have nibbled on the rope and somehow got it untied."

Axel stepped around him. The rope was perfectly intact. If the horse hadn't untied it, someone had. But it didn't look chewed on. He scanned the ground for any unusual prints. Nothing. Just his boots and his father's. Plus, the filly looked to have taken her sweet time, touring the area and visiting with the other horses before striking out to the west...toward Cooper land. He'd best be getting after her if he didn't want to stir any pots.

"What you thinking?"

Axel moved past to fetch the saddle and bridle from the barn for his gelding. "I don't know. I have a hard time believing she got those knots loose on her own. But there's nothing here to suggest otherwise."

Pa followed slower. Axel shot him a glance to find him scratching the side of his jaw, looking thoughtful.

"What are *you* thinking?" Axel asked

"Awe, nothing." Pa waved him away. "Just an unfortunate chance, I reckon. You go after her while I finish the chores and start on breakfast. You'll probably be back before Luke gets here, but if not, I'll send him out to help."

At least that brightened the situation. Old Luke Ingles came down every Sunday, and if Axel had any trouble finding Desert Lady, there wasn't anything the old mountain man couldn't track. With any luck he'd also be able to tell who untied the rope, because Axel was pretty sure the filly hadn't managed that on her own.

But it was just the kind of mischief the Cooper boys might try.

Chapter 6

Now was her chance. Elizabeth didn't even bother changing from her nightgown. With the Forsbergs distracted by the missing horse, she should have time to search the large trunk. The shawl wrapping her shoulders, she hurried to Lars's room and heaved the large lid open. Clothes sat on top, clean and folded with care. Then a couple of woolen blankets. A stack of books rose from one side. On the other, an old pair of boots nestled the corner while a wooden box, no more than six inches tall and a foot long, rested along the back. A large lock sealed it.

The money.

Why else would it be so fortified and hidden out of sight? She had to get it open, but a thorough examination of the rest of the trunk revealed no key and she didn't remember seeing one during her search of the cabin. No matter. If she couldn't get in through the front, she'd find another way.

Elizabeth carried the box to the table, then slipped to the window to make sure she still had time. There was no sign of Axel, but Lars was already half way to the cabin.

Grabbing the box, she darted back to the trunk, but paused before setting it in. A weathered envelope lay on the floor of the trunk, thick with letters or documents. She snatched it out, dropped the box in place, piled the blankets and clothes back on top, lowered the lid, and raced back to Axel's room. The door clicked closed as the one at the front of the cabin opened. Elizabeth leaned into the wood to catch her breath while Lars walked to the stove. Hinges sang. He was probably stoking the fire so he could heat some coffee or make breakfast. Probably both.

Tiptoeing away from the door, Elizabeth tossed her shawl to the bed and hurried to dress. As she brushed the tangles from her hair, the aroma of frying eggs and steak leaked into the room, making her stomach ache. These men loved their beef. She would miss their cooking when she left, but at least she would have the means of eating well once she got that box open.

"Good morning," Lars greeted as she stepped out of the bedroom. "Sorry about the ruckus earlier. Axel's gone after the filly, and I doubt he'll have too much trouble bringing her home."

"Good." Elizabeth pasted a smile on her face. The last thing she needed was for him to suspect her. Not until she was ready to leave. The thought of the locked box hidden in the next room was enough to twinge each nerve in her body. "Is there anything I can do to help?" She'd play the part of Eliza a while longer.

"If you want to set plates out, I'd like to talk with you about something."

"Of course." Though she didn't want to hear anything he had to say, she walked to the shelves and pulled three of the metal plates from where they had been left to dry after supper. Her gaze wandered to the finer china on a higher shelf, an elegant rose design adorning the border.

"Those were Axel's mother's." Lars sighed and returned his focus to flipping the eggs. "We didn't bring much with us when we left New York, but there were a few things of hers we couldn't let go of."

Elizabeth remained silent and set the plates out on the table.

"Besides," Lars continued, "it makes this wilderness feel more like a home. Here, hand me one of those."

She passed him a plate, and he loaded it with eggs.

"I want to apologize for not being completely honest with you about those letters I sent. I didn't want to deceive you, but I knew Axel would never do it for himself. He'd waste his life away up here and never realize what he was missing until he died alone. He never thinks beyond this ranch, it's been his dream for so long. But I wanted more for him than that." Lars set the spatula aside and took one of her hands. "Will you forgive me?"

Forgive him? Elizabeth struggled with the instinct to yank away. "Of course." Perhaps for that one offence, but not for destroying her family. She would never forgive that.

"Thank you."

She turned away before her face betrayed her. It was too hard to keep the hate from twisting down the corners of her mouth, or lighting a fire in her eyes.

"I believe with all my soul that Axel will be a good husband to you if you let him. His mother raised him well—I can take no credit for that. I was always gone when he was young. I had decided when we came to America that I would take full advantage of all opportunities while here. I would make us wealthy. I gave everything to that goal. And then Camilla died."

Was he trying to explain why he felt justified in his misuse of her father? Perhaps he was right about Axel, and the younger Forsberg didn't deserve to be the brunt of her wrath...but she couldn't think of a way to injure the elder without hurting his son in the process. And why should she try? Her father hadn't been the only one harmed by Lars's actions.

Elizabeth pushed away every sensation of feeling while she sat and ate, clearing her plate before Axel shoved his way into the cabin with a white haired, unbathed man in buckskin clothes on his heels. A full beard didn't hide the grin on the man's face. "Well, I'll be! When Axel told me he'd gotten married, I laughed in his face, figuring he'd come off that horse of his one too many times, but I see I was a little hasty with my assumptions."

Axel's lips pulled up a little, but his brow remained furrowed. "Eliza, this is Luke Ingles. Luke, this is my wife."

"The Good Lord must love you, son," Luke swept his sweat-stained hat off and nodded to Elizabeth, "because He usually don't send angels to mingle with the likes of us."

Axel allowed himself a smile, but he was still visibly ready to boil over.

Elizabeth pressed her hands to her side as the tension continued to build along her spine.

"A pleasure to meet you, Mr. Ingles. Were you able to find your horse, Axel?"

"Yes." The terseness of his tone told exactly how he felt about the whole ordeal.

"Good."

He tromped to the table and braced his hands against the edge. "Pa, Luke agrees with me. There's no way that horse untied those knots with no marks on the ropes. I don't know how they got in and out with no prints, but it's got to be the Coopers. This is just the thing that youngest boy, Eli, would do."

Lars dished up a steak and some eggs and slid the plate toward his son. "But with no prints, of any kind—"

"Luke and I talked about that." Axel sat down and picked up a fork while Lars fixed another plate for the mountain man. "He said he's seen it before where someone wraps his feet and horse's hooves with rags. It would make it harder to find the tracks, but we'll take another look after breakfast."

"There's no hurry," the older man said, hunkering down in the chair next to Axel. "If the tracks are there, they won't go anywhere before we're done with meeting."

Elizabeth looked to each man in turn, coming to the slow realization of what Mr. Ingles was talking about. A Bible sat at the far corner of the table and today was Sunday. What excuse could she use to avoid what must be coming?

***

Axel glanced to the door, his leg involuntarily twitching his desire to walk out as Pa continued to read from the New Testament.

"'Let all bitterness, and wrath, and anger, and clamor, and evil speaking, be put away from you, with all malice.'"

He'd read one scripture after another about forgiveness, and now he had moved on to putting away anger. Not something Axel wanted to do quite yet. He'd get around to that after he rode up to the Cooper ranch.

"'And be ye kind one to another, tenderhearted, forgiving one another, even as God for Christ's sake hath forgiven you.'"

Axel glanced to Eliza and the stoic look on her face. Did she understand his need to face the Coopers about releasing the horse, or was she, as a good Christian woman, in agreement with Pa that he should let it go, turn the other cheek? She'd likely think less of him for holding a grudge.

He let out his breath and slumped in his chair, drawing everyone's attention. "What?"

Luke laughed out loud and leaned to clap Axel on the back. "Your Pa is one for his sermons, isn't he? Doesn't say a word. Pulls out that Bible and has you repenting six ways from Sunday."

Axel grunted his reply. "All right. I'll leave the Coopers alone. But I'll be waiting for them. Next time they sneak over here with their tomfoolery, I won't let it go."

"We don't even know that it was them." Pa lowered the Bible to his lap, but it remained open.

"Who else would it be? I know that horse didn't let herself go."

"Just don't go rushing off when you're angry. If we need to talk to them, we'll both ride up in the middle of the day. And we'll leave the guns at home. I don't care if it is Harvey's boys having themselves a laugh, we don't need a feud on our hands."

Axel crossed his arms and stole another glance at Eliza. Pa was right. He couldn't let his anger drive him to risk his life when he had a wife to provide for. He had a responsibility to her now. What's more, he didn't want her regretting the man she'd married. He'd told her he wasn't given to losing his temper, and yet she'd only been here two days and already she'd seen it flare. Thankfully, she didn't look upset as she met his gaze. Instead she appeared contemplative...and almost pleased. A spark lit her eyes as she gave him a small smile.

***

Elizabeth sat on the edge of the bed and unfolded the documents that had been crammed into the aged envelope. She paused to listen, but as far as she could tell the men still loitered outside discussing the ranch and swapping tales with Luke Ingles. She pulled the lamp near, the lowering sun no longer providing sufficient light to make out the tiny type-set words. It was a document of some kind. Involving the business, outlining equal shared interests and dated seventeen years ago. She flipped to the next paper. Pushing aside the several handwritten letters in between. Another form outlined the sale of fifty percent of the business by Lars Forsberg to her father. For the sum of four dollars and twenty-three cents.

Was it a joke of some sorts? Had this been mockery of Father after Forsberg had already taken everything from the business? Why else would he have kept the document but to humor himself at the memory of his successful swindle? She folded the papers and shoved them back in the envelope, her stomach churning. Lars Forsberg was the worst kind of scoundrel. He had sat with his Bible today and spouted scripture to control his son. He had looked at her with such genuine apology and asked for her forgiveness. No wonder Father had been taken in by him.

She almost felt sorry for Axel.

Elizabeth wrapped the envelope in the clothes she'd worn that day and stuffed the bundle into her trunk. At the first opportunity, she would return it to the trunk in Lars's room. Then she would try to figure out a way into the box. And how to start a war.

At the sound of the men entering the cabin, Elizabeth jumped into the bed and jerked the quilt over her. A moment later, the bedroom door sighed open. Axel moved across the room, momentarily pausing at the foot of the bed to remove his boots and outside clothes. She remained facing away as he crawled onto the mattress beside her. For a couple of minutes he laid silent, then his callused hand squeezed her shoulder, and he pressed his lips to her ear.

"I'm sorry."

Elizabeth rotated onto her back and peered up at him. Lamplight lit the angles of his face and glowed in his eyes. Her breathing slowed. "For what?"

He lowered himself beside her, forcing her to turn a little farther if she wanted to see his face. She couldn't help herself. Even though he softened his voice, it rumbled. "I was thinking about your letters. After Pa asked you about your faith in Christ, you wrote with such devotion. I can't help wondering how disappointed you must be realizing you've married a flawed man."

Elizabeth stared at him, the earnestness in his gaze, the tight line his mouth formed. Her heart seemed to seize. As did her mind. "I...I don't..."

"You don't have to say anything."

Didn't she? Make up some line? Continue her charade? "Aren't we all flawed?" Her whispered words rang loud in her head as did her mother's, ones Elizabeth had heard spoken at home and at church as a child. "Isn't that why we need Christ?"

A crease appeared in his cheek as though he considered a smile. His gaze moved to her lips and in slow motion Axel leaned nearer until his mouth covered hers with a gentle kiss.

Chapter 7

"Has anyone seen my watch?"

Elizabeth glanced at Lars. He stood in the doorway to his bedroom patting his pockets.

Seated at the table, Axel pulled on his boots. "Nope."

Elizabeth shook her head as she set the stack of dirty breakfast dishes into the basin and the embrace of hot water. She kept her motions slow. Finally, Lars made a sound in the back of his throat and went outside.

Axel set a hat on his head, his gaze on her. "Like I said, we'll probably be gone 'til after dark. The steers are up on the high pasture, and it'll take time to move them lower. Are you sure there's nothing you need before we leave?"

Elizabeth paused before giving her answer. It wouldn't do to sound too anxious for them to go. "No. I'll be fine. There is plenty for me to keep myself busy with, and I am quite used to taking care of myself."

Axel nodded, but his face still showed unease. He took a step forward. Paused. Then two more steps to where she stood. Hesitation showed in his eyes and movements, but he set a kiss to her forehead. "Have a good day." He spun and hurried out of the cabin.

Elizabeth stared after him even as the door closed, an ache rising in her chest, like an icepick chipping at the corners of her heart. Ever since his kiss a week and a half earlier... Axel had gradually deepened it until she'd finally found the presence of mind to roll away from him. He'd laid down and fallen asleep quite quickly, but she'd stared into the darkness for hours, her lips still tingling from the touch of his. Like living one of her childhood fantasies.

Elizabeth swatted at the memory like a pesky fly. She wouldn't let herself think of that kiss anymore, or what it did to her insides. Wiping her hands on a towel, she hurried to the door and cracked it open just enough to see where Axel approached his father. They both mounted their horses. As soon as they rode from sight, Elizabeth pressed the door closed and strode into Lars's bedroom. Finally. There'd never been opportunity before—enough time alone with the box and whatever was inside without the fear of being caught.

With both men gone, Elizabeth brought the box to the table and examined it from every angle. Solid wood construction. A large lock. And hinges located on the inside. Maybe she needed to look for the key again.

An hour turned up nothing but more frustration. She would have to find a way to force her way in. An overcast sky hung above her as she darted to the barn. A collection of tools hung on the wall not far from the tack for the horses. Elizabeth hefted a large hammer, and then selected two sizes of chisels. Back in the cabin, the hammer only dented the lock. There was no way in without taking the box itself apart. Not ideal, but she needed that money.

Taking up the larger of the chisels, Elizabeth wedged it under the lid and laid the hammer to it. The money had to be in there. As soon as she had the funds, she would be able to start her new life. She'd finish with the Forsbergs and be gone. The dry wood began to splinter as the thick steel sank inside. A crack appeared along the top. Her hands trembling with anticipation, she wedged the slimmer chisel in the tiny gap and gave it a hard hit. The crevasse extended the length of the lid. She torqued on both chisels, ripping the box open and bearing its contents.

Heart pumping, Elizabeth dug out the bobbins of colored thread, pin cushion, a doily, two books of poetry, a small silken pouch, and decorative hair pins. The items were soon spread across the table, the box emptied. No purses of gold and silver, or banknotes. Nothing.

She dropped into a chair as her chest constricted, choking her heart.

No.

Now what? If she couldn't find the money, she'd be stuck in this place—worse off than the sewing factory and drafty apartment in New York.

Then she thought of Axel's warm bed, his cooking...and his kiss. Not quite worse off. Except she was supposed to hate him and her life here was a deception.

No. She jerked to her feet, her hands dancing over the contents of the box. There had to be something besides memorabilia. Keepsakes from Lar's dead wife. That's all this was. Elizabeth's breath came in short gasps.

No!

There had to be something. She craned her neck, bringing her head up to search the cabin with her eyes. Where hadn't she looked? She'd hunted everywhere. Even the barn. Every nook and cranny. Nothing. Had they buried it? That seemed the only option left, which meant she'd never find it. Not in a thousand years unless they told her where it was. But how likely was that? How could she ask without drawing suspicion?

"Curse you, Forsbergs!" She gave the basin across from her an angry shove, and it toppled over the edge of the table with a crash as tin dishes collided. Water rushed across the floor, puddling in places, and soaking into others. "I hate you."

Elizabeth moaned, sinking back into the chair. "And I hate myself for coming here. For thinking I was clever."

What a fool she'd turned out to be. She just wanted to leave this place. To go home. Except she didn't really have one of those anymore.

Elizabeth reached out and toyed with the silk pouch. A beautiful rosy color but too small to hold much of anything. Still, she'd look to be sure. She loosened the ribbon cinching the opening and shook the pouch over her palm. A ring and a brooch tumbled from their cocoon.

The brooch was a lovely emerald arrangement set in silver. Certainly worth enough to get where she needed to, but it paled beside the ring. A large, deep blue gem encircled by elegant etching of silver and placement of diamonds. Even exquisite didn't seem sufficient a word. No doubt Axel's mother had also left this behind. The ring now represented a new life for Elizabeth, far away from Axel and his father. Only...taking a ring, an heirloom most likely, seemed closer to stealing than taking money she already considered stolen. Elizabeth hooked the tip of her finger through the band, strength slipping away. How weary she was of all this. She just wanted the ordeal, the lies, and the pretense to be over.

What other choice had she but to take the ring?

Elizabeth glanced to the shelf and the tin of matches. Then stood. Her hands trembled as she gathered everything back into the box then set the broken pieces of lid on top. Hopefully, buried deep in the trunk, Lars would not notice anything amiss until she was far from here.

***

Axel propped the saddle against the wall and hooked the bridle on a peg. A yawn watered his eyes as he turned from the barn and started to the house. Well past midnight, his muscles ached and his body begged for sleep. His thoughts hazed, his mind already succumbing to exhaustion. Even still, he paused at the well to wash up a little, something he wouldn't have bothered with before he shared a bed, before it mattered if the bedding smelled like horse.

Inside the cabin, Pa had a lamp lit, and it cast a light across the clean floor. Very clean. Eliza had kept busy today. A good sign she was adjusting to this wilderness and making herself at home. Some of the tension building over the past week eased from his shoulders. Eliza had seemed detached from everything since she'd come, as if a tangible barrier stood between her and calling this place home. On the surface, she'd helped around the cabin, and spent a lot of time with her little mare, but her eyes—though deep enough to draw him in every time he looked at her—remained distant. And a little sad. Axel nodded toward Pa and turned into his own bedroom.

Another yawn stretched his mouth as he crawled between the covers after undressing. He wiped his hand down his face. Eliza shifted beside him.

"I'm sorry," he whispered.

She didn't face him but turned her head slightly. "For what?"

"Waking you."

Her head shook. "I wasn't asleep yet."

Axel pushed up on an elbow. Had she

waited up for him...or was she simply not at ease alone in the cabin? Could he hope that maybe she'd worried for him? A little? He resisted the need to wrap her in his arms. He'd settle for a quick kiss to her temple. For now.

As always, she stiffened at his touch.

He laid back down. "Good night."

No reply. Maybe he would get used to her silence someday.

He closed his eyes and pressed his hands over them. Time. He had to give her time. The woman who wrote those letters was buried in there somewhere. There were moments he saw glimpses of humor, and even warmth.

"Eliza?"

"What?"

"Would you consider riding with me tomorrow? I could show you more of the ranch. Desert Lady needs exercise, and Stitches would probably enjoy the companionship." As would he. If only he could be certain she felt the same.

Silence filled the room. He could almost hear the minutes tick away in his head. It felt as though any hope of a happy future with her hung on her reply.

"All right."

He released his breath and settled into his pillow.

Chapter 8

Elizabeth sat up and glanced to Axel's still form. Only moments after his last words, he became like a log beside her, completely unconscious to the world. Strange how familiar she'd already become with his breathing. Even stranger to see him lying there, completely unaware and defenseless. How was it her enemy could tug at her heart?

She hurried to collect Axel's boots and the envelope of documents she'd found in the trunk—the mockery of Father's devastation—then fled the room. Elizabeth refused to think about Axel tonight. At all. His exhaustion would only aid her. She focused her thoughts on Lars instead, his Sunday services about love and healing—flowery words burning like salt on her open wounds. She hated him all the more for them. The tin of matches waited for her on the shelf.

The quarter moon gave just enough light to

make her way across the yard before she plunged into the darkness of the barn. Elizabeth pushed the door open wide to allow for some sight. She needed to make sure the building was empty. Only one of the stalls was being used, and she hurried to release the horse, chasing the animal outside. Then turned back and glanced around. All sat silent in shadow. Empty but for the stack of hay near the back and the tack for the wagon and horses near the front.

That was a problem.

How was she going to leave if all the saddles and bridles burned too? She made a pile of them a ways from the door. Then returned inside with the papers and matches. She struck the match on the box then held the flame to the corner on the envelope. She pictured Mother's last days, still hearing the cough that ripped apart her lungs. The feeling of complete helplessness. Both would always haunt her. As would the image of Mother lying motionless, face bereft of any color or life.

"I just wish I could bring you back."

Elizabeth dropped the flame onto the stack of hay and made her retreat. She ran the distance to the cabin, the large boots chaffing her legs. Kicking them off at the door, she glanced behind. The whole interior seemed to glow and the horses in the nearest corral began to whinny. She had to get back in bed before they woke the Forsbergs.

Heart beating a steady clip, Elizabeth sprinted on her bare toes across the large room and into the one she shared with Axel. She set his boots back in place and slipped beneath his mother's quilt. He gave a soft moan as he rolled. And draped his arm over her. Elizabeth clamped her teeth and tried not to move, to pretend to sleep. She could very well imagine what they might do to her if they knew what she'd done.

Axel's breath warmed her neck as his chest slowed its movements. He'd fallen back asleep. Or maybe he'd never really woken up. That would explain the arm. Axel had done well at keeping his word to let her dictate the timing of their relationship. Other than that single kiss, he'd been very much a gentleman. Kind. Considerate. And she'd just lit his barn on fire.

Elizabeth released a moan of her own. What if Axel had nothing to do with his father's theft? What if he didn't even know about it? Would she destroy him to get even with Lars? Was there any other way?

No.

Still, the weight of his arm over her laid heavy. Like her guilt.

A minute later, Elizabeth couldn't let herself stay silent while everything burned. Maybe he would be able to save something, or at least make sure the horses and the rest of the ranch stayed safe.

"Axel?"

His arm tightened around her and he sighed.

"Axel, wake up." She rotated to him and gave him a shake.

***

Axel fought the grogginess, opening his eyes to the dim outline of Eliza. A slight glow lit the window. Was it dawn already?

"The horses, Axel. Listen. I think something is scaring the horses."

The franticness of her tone jerked him awake and he sat up. Anxious whinnies pulled him the rest of the way to his feet and he yanked on his pants, boots, and raced into the front yard, arriving about the same time as Pa. Flames lapped at the walls of the barn.

"Who...?" Axel couldn't say any more as the muscles in his jaw tightened. Who could it be but the Coopers?

Pa tugged him from his anger. "The front part still looks sturdy enough. If we hurry, we might be able to save something."

Axel ran with him, stumbling over a saddle in the middle of the yard. A whole heap of tack and other equipment. But why on earth...?

No time. He passed by and plunged into the furnace that had been their barn. He grabbed an armful of tools from inside the door and retreated. The night appeared twice as dark after facing the brilliance of the flames, but he emptied his load with the pile of saddles and bridles, and turned back.

Pa caught his sleeve. "Don't worry about more. It's getting too dangerous. Let's move the horses to the farthest corral and away from the heat."

With a nod Axel followed, but not before glancing to where Eliza stood in her nightgown and bare feet at the front of the cabin. The blaze consuming the barn illuminated the horror on her face. His chest constricted over his winded lungs. This was the sort of thing to scare a woman like her away, make her want to leave, and he'd hardly be able to blame her. He might even encourage it. The need to protect her washed over him with overwhelming force. First the missing horse. Now the barn. What next? Would he be able to keep her safe?

Anger and fear mingled in an unfamiliar way as he helped with the anxious horses. A loud moan drowned out the roar of the flames, and a gust of searing air blew across the yard. The roof gave way and crashed inwards. Axel's stomach churned at the thought of how many hours, and how much labor, had been put into felling each tree and splitting each log. Not to mention the cost of nails and hinges. And all he could do was stand back and watch it be reduced to a pile of rubble.

Axel looked back to the cabin, but Eliza had already gone back inside. He found her in their bed, quilt tucked around her, but eyes open and staring. He sat beside her and braced her shoulder. "Are you all right?"

Her head gave a little shake.

"Eliza..." Axel blew out his breath, ready to buckle on his revolver and pay a visit to the Coopers. Why did this have to happen now, with his bride barely off the stagecoach? He toed off his boots and laid down beside her. He opened his arms. "Come here."

"Axel, no." She started to turn away.

"It's all right." He drew her to him and held on as her body shivered. "We'll find out who did this." And heaven help that man.

After Eliza relaxed and appeared to be resting, Axel slipped away and back outside. Dawn lit the east and stretched its rays across the valley. Pa hauled the tack and tools they'd saved to the side of the cabin.

"Why would someone remove the saddles before lighting it on fire?" The one thing that didn't make any sense to Axel.

"Maybe the fire was an accident?"

"What? You think the Cooper boys were fooling around and didn't mean to light it?" A part of Axel wanted them guilty of more than just trespassing.

"We don't know that the Coopers are responsible."

Axel wanted to laugh out loud. "Who else could it have been? We haven't had trouble with anyone else in the area."

Pa glanced to the door of the cabin and then to the vestiges of the barn, a smoldering heap. "Let's not rush in to any confrontations until we're sure. I looked around already and I didn't see any extra tracks in the area, but hopefully the smoke will bring Luke down so he can search as well."

"And if it is the Coopers?" Axel tapped his hand to his leg. No matter what Pa said, he wasn't going up there unarmed.

***

"Eliza?"

Her whole body tensed as she glanced to

Lars. "Yes?" She kept her hands busy with the dishes, rinsing dinner from them.

"Don't let the fire bother you. I think Axel is afraid it will scare you away, but I think you're a stronger woman than that."

A spec of roast clung to a fork, and she added more force to her scrubbing. Something in his voice knotted her shoulders. As though he suspected... "Thank you."

"Axel is becoming quite fond of you." His tone softened, becoming almost a plea. "I suspect he might be falling in love."

Love? Instead of feeling flattered, or elated that she was so successful at her revenge, Elizabeth's insides twisted. Her motions slowed as the tender feelings of her childhood infatuation with Axel squeezed her heart.

She'd been caught in her own web.

Chapter 9

Two days later, Axel grinned as he encouraged Desert Lady forward. She lengthened her stride, tearing dry sod. She raced across the meadow as smooth as the breeze on his face. The past week had only landed him on his rear once as he worked with her, gaining her trust and giving her more in return. He still braced himself for the chance she might startle or decide to help him disembark, but no longer believed she was out to break every last bone in his body.

As he reached the stand of trees bordering the grassland, Axel slowed Lady's gait and glanced behind at the other female who had become a part of his life. Eliza. Her gray mare loped past the cluster of cattle at the edge of the stream, following his course. He appreciated the moment to watch her. And to remember what it had felt like to kiss her that once. Unfortunately, the memory dimmed with each passing day. As she rode toward him, the sun on her face, he wanted nothing more than to remind himself of the taste and feel of her lips. If only she would let him. But where she'd been withdrawn before the fire, the two days since had pulled her further from him. The only time she let him near was for that brief moment when they retired for the night and he touched her arm to press a kiss to her temple. After that, he'd rolled over and tried to sleep. An increasingly difficult task with her so close.

How long would it take to win her trust, as well?

Maybe out here, away from the reminders of the fire.

Eliza's breath came in bursts as she pulled her horse alongside his. "I thought I'd lost you. Lady should be racing instead of herding cows."

"Perhaps, but I think she'll prefer it up here. Neither of us were meant for the city or gawking crowds."

She nudged Stitches past and into the woods. Axel followed. Most of the trees were pine or cypress, but the few others showed the approach of autumn. Yellow blended with shades of green. They followed the stream, still flowing steady despite July and August giving less rain than most years.

"What about you?" Axel asked as he caught up. "Do you like it here? I know how different it is from New York."

"It is that."

"And? You don't want to go back, do you?" The thought of her leaving tromped over him like stampeding cows. He'd seen it happen time and time again. A man came out west with his wife, or sent for a woman when he got settled, and after a while the loneliness and wildness of the area became too much for her. The missing horse, the fire. Another incident like that might drive Eliza away, and that would make him angrier with the Coopers than the loss of the barn.

Silence. Maybe he needed to find out what else, besides the Coopers, he was up against.

"What do you miss the most?" he asked.

She glanced to him. "When I left New York I had little to call my own, never mind miss. But if I looked back further...music. I used to love the piano." Her gaze dropped to her fingers draped over the saddle horn, the leather rein woven between. "I probably wouldn't even remember how to play anymore."

One more loss she'd endured. "You said in your letters that your parents had both died. Do you have any other kin back East?"

"No."

"How young were you when they passed?" It was strange to think of her as an orphan, but she'd never volunteered any information about her childhood.

"I was fourteen when my mother died. She'd been ill for months."

Axel had been eighteen by the time sickness took his own mother. How much more the loss would have affected a young girl?

"Seventeen when Father followed."

"And you've been on your own since." He reached out and patted Stitches' rump, recalling what Eliza had said about the sewing factory.

"Yes." Her voice hardened, but she stared at the flowing water, keeping her gaze completely averted from him, making it impossible to read her expression.

"Then you would rather live here? You wouldn't want to leave."

A wren left its perch on a nearby branch and flitted across their path. Lady shook her head with a snort then settled.

"Eliza?"

"No." Her spine straightened but her shoulders seemed to slump. She glanced back. "No, I don't want to leave." Her heels rammed Stiches ribs, and the gray mare lurched forward then spun as Eliza yanked the reins to the side, forcing her around and past Axel toward the meadow.

"What's wrong?"

"I'm tired. I'm going back to the cabin."

Axel watched her. As usual, Eliza wanted to be alone, and she'd make it home easily enough. To be sure, he followed to the trail. Then, instead of turning right as she had, he reined left, an idea forming. With the barn in ashes, now was not the time to spend money, but he wanted Eliza to be happy here. Though Desert Lady was a little balky since she'd lost her partner, a long ride would work some of that out of her, and he could be back in a couple of hours.

Anticipation surged through Axel, and he encouraged Lady to a faster clip. He'd buy Eliza something nice. As long as Captain Gray wasn't out on patrol with his men, he'd be able to get into the safe at the cavalry office and send the money to Phoenix with Sam.

Axel glanced at the sun, almost directly above him. If he hurried, he might catch the stage and be able to discuss his plan with Sam in person. The man owed him a favor, and Axel couldn't think of a better time to collect.

He'd order nails for a new barn while he was at it.

***

Elizabeth melted onto the bed, her hand slipping to the indent on Axel's pillow where his head rested each night...so close to hers. How was it possible to be so affected by a man? One she was supposed to despise. Since she'd stepped off the stagecoach and saw him standing there, her heart had been drawn to him. Just as it had as a young girl, only seeing him once every twelve months.

But Lars was still responsible for all her losses. She had to leave, and had the means to do it and a plan in place. She couldn't stop now. Her hand was set to the plow. Just like the scripture.

Oh, why couldn't other scriptures have penetrated her as that one had? Ones like Lars read to them and old Luke the last two Sundays. Why couldn't she believe in forgiveness and grace? Or in a God who cared for her? They had seemed easy concepts before Mother's...

Elizabeth pressed the heels of her hands into her eyes trying to blot out the memories of her mother's final days, wasted away to not much more than a skeleton, her cough persistent, keeping everyone from sleep in the long hours of the night. Blood staining the once white handkerchiefs and their delicate lace.

Rolling off the bed onto her knees, Elizabeth crawled to the chest holding all she had left of her past. She drew out its contents one by one. Under her own modest clothes lay Mother's lace shawl and matching gloves rolled together. She slipped the first over her head, and then pulled the gloves up her arms to her elbows. Next came Father's cigar box with his old pocket watch and a hair comb with pale pink roses. And at the very bottom, their family Bible. Every important date recorded within its cover. Every birth, death and marriage of the Landviks for the past hundred years. Elizabeth let her finger, veiled in the intricate weave of threads, trace over the entries, pausing over the last two—the ones she had written herself.

She let her eyes close. They remained dry, but her chest ached with such awful pain.

Chapter 10

Elizabeth stared at the door and the perfect square of light glowing through the window. The half-moon would make it easier to find her way across the countryside. *If* she followed through with her plan. She stilled her breath to listen to the slow rhythm of Axel's. She wished she could close her eyes and fall asleep. She'd wake in the morning, no longer Elizabeth Landvick. Axel need never know the truth. She could stay Eliza Forsberg...

And spend her life hating herself and Lars. What if Axel someday learned who she was? How long could she bury her identity....as she had her parents. Wouldn't that be the greatest betrayal of all?

She slipped from the bed.

Elizabeth quietly dressed, her clothes prepared, but didn't put on her shoes until she'd stepped outside and closed the door. The night sat silent. Even the crickets slept. One of the horses gave a low nicker as she approached with Stitches' bridle. The little mare stood as Elizabeth slipped the bit into her mouth. The saddle was so much heavier than Axel made it appear, but at least he had showed her how to fasten the straps. Finally, she pulled herself onto Stitches back and reined her toward the trail leading to the Coopers.

As Elizabeth rode, she rehearsed every memory of her parents, fortifying her resolve to follow through. Mother's tears as she wrapped the last of her jewels, even heirlooms, and sold them to pay off Father's debts. The crates filled with everything they owned lining the walls of their empty home. The drafty apartment in an unsavory part of town. Thin walls and dirty hallways.

Elizabeth followed the trail a ways before the homestead came into view with barns and a couple of large stacks of hay. A low light shone from the open door on the main barn. Someone was probably there. Reining Stitches to the edge of the trail, Elizabeth dismounted. Her pulse sped. Two huge haystacks blocked her from being seen from the cabin. They would have to do. Leading Stitches after her, Elizabeth crept toward the first stack, pulling Lar's timepiece from her pocket. She dropped it and continued on. Her hand fumbled with the matchbox as she struggled to forget the look on Axel's face at the sight of the burning barn—before the rage had appeared.

"Axel." Elizabeth gritted her teeth and lit a match. There was no way to hurt Lars without Axel feeling some of the sting.

But what if she took it too far?

What was she doing? She blew out the match. The Coopers hadn't even done anything to her family, and yet here she stood, about to burn their hay and start a war.

We are ruined. Forsberg has destroyed us. He's left us with nothing. There's no money left. The business, the house, everything. It's lost.

Her father's sobs surrounded her in the darkness as they had every night trying to sleep in that box of a room, alone because Mother was dead and Father didn't bother coming home until dawn arrived and he'd drunk away what little he'd earned the day before.

Elizabeth struck another match. She stared at the tiny flame cradling the tip. All she had to do was let go. The hay would burn. A feud would begin. And she'd make her escape with the ring and brooch.

The flicker of orange and red crept down the thin splinter of wood. How could she do this to Axel? What if something happened to him? Should he pay for his father's sins?

She could walk away now. Isn't that what Lars kept reading to them from the Bible? The Bible that had once been a part of her life. Mother had believed. Even at the end.

Elizabeth pressed her eyes closed. "Oh, God. Please. Let me forgive. I don't want to hate anymore. Help me walk away before I hurt him again."

Searing pain bit her fingers, and she jerked her hand, releasing the match. Her eyes flew open to see the flame sink into the loose hay...and spread.

"No."

She stamped her boot over the flame. Again and again, fighting the growing blaze as Stitches tried to jerk away, almost pulling her off balance. Heat pricked her legs. Her hem lit the darkness. With a yelp she stumbled back and hit her knees, somehow keeping hold on the rein while smothering the flame in the dirt.

Stitches continued to toss her head and pull back.

"Easy." Elizabeth got her to hold still long enough to climb into the saddle.

"Who goes there?" a man hollered from the barn. The discharge of a gun and then the cry of "fire!" perforated the night. Stitches needed no encouragement in racing toward home. The pungent smell of the horse's sweat filled Elizabeth's senses by time she slowed the animal on Forsberg land. She would need to brush the lathered coat well before putting Stitches back in the corral. She would also need to wash herself and hide her scorched dress.

***

The mattresses shifted and something cold touched his leg, drawing him out of sleep.

"Eliza?"

She stilled. "Yes?" The word wavered.

He blinked the weariness from his eyes and touched her arm. Her skin felt chill through the thin linen sleeve. "Come here." Axel wrapped her close and she complied, but trembled. "What's wrong?"

"A nightmare."

He tightened his hold. If only he could protect her from them, as well. He turned her toward him. Axel cupped her cheek, brushing his thumb over her lips, barely visible with the sun still below the horizon. Dare he? Before his weary mind could decide, her lips touched his. Just as quickly she withdrew and rotated away from him.

Every ounce of weariness fled. "Eliza?"

"Go to sleep, Axel."

That might have been possible before she'd kissed him. But now... He leaned closer, so his face touched her braided hair. He pressed his mouth to her neck. "Eliza. Is there nothing I can do for you?"

"You can go to sleep." Yet even as she said the words, her body eased against his.

Taking courage, Axel slipped his hand along her waist and across her stomach, gradually turning her back toward him. She gave, and he maneuvered his arm, and then shoulder, under her head. She looked up, and the first ray of dawn touched the room, and her eyes. They closed as he guided her chin with the tips of his fingers. Their mouths met.

As their kiss lengthened, Axel's chest tightened until it hurt. The need to hold her, protect her, and love her, gripped him and lit the ends of each nerve. She was his wife. They would work together, laugh together, and raise a family. He would give her his life. And never let her go. His hand slid up her back to her head as he rotated above her. His fingers pressed under her pillow. Pain bit the tips.

He yanked his hand away and broke the kiss. "What was...?" Droplets of crimson trickled down his hand.

Her eyes widened as he rolled off of her. "What happened?" She pushed up onto her elbows, and he yanked the pillow away.

A knife.

"Eliza?" Axel balled his hand so the pressure of his palm would stanch the bleeding. "Why do you have a knife?"

Her expression hardened as she scrambled to her feet and backed away from the bed.

"What would you need a knife for?" He sat back with a glance to where she had been laying—where *they* had been laying. "What sort of marriage did you want this to be?"

"I didn't want a marriage." She spoke so suddenly and so softly, he almost missed her words. Eliza's hands pressed against her cheeks.

Axel stared, the wind knocked out of him. "But you said... W—why would you come here...and marry me...if..." And how did the knife fit in? "Did you plan to kill me in my sleep, or just threaten me if I got to close to you? I don't understand, Eliza. If you didn't want a marriage, why—"

"I'm not who you think I am."

"You didn't write those letters?"

Instead of answering, she sank against the wall, and then to the floor.

Axel straightened, grinding his teeth. "Then who are you?" He shifted his gaze to the knife. His boots sat where he left them at the foot of the bed. No prints were ever found after Desert Lady was released or the barn burned. And he'd never made sense of that stack of saddles outside the burning barn. His gut clenched. "It was you?" The rattlesnake had been in their bedroll all along.

When she remained mute, he turned his back to pull his clothes on and thrust his feet in each boot. Eliza, or whatever her name was, never moved. Just sat there expressionless. Like she had no feeling in her. But still just as pretty as ever with dark strands of hair free from her braid, laid across her white face. He needed some distance to sort the pieces of this puzzle. He plunged out of the bedroom.

Pa was already awake and started a fire in the stove. He looked up, the lamp lighting his curious brow. "Axel?"

"If you can take care of the chores here, I'm riding out to check on the cattle. Don't let..." he thrust a finger toward the bedroom, "*that woman* out of your sight 'til I get back." He wrapped his cut fingers and snatched his gun belt from its hook, buckling it on. Then collected his saddle and bridle from the floor.

The morning air greeted Axel with a breeze that nipped at the sweat on his forehead. His anger only increased at the blackened remains of the barn. He trotted to the corral where his gelding waited. Dessert Lady could sit tight for now. The last thing he need this morning was to be thrown onto a dung pile by another female.

Chapter 11

He was gone. Still there were no tears. Just the pain radiating from her center as it had when Mother, and then Father, left. Elizabeth touched a finger against her lips as she closed her eyes to relive that moment in Axel's arms. The sun streamed through the window before she struggled to her feet, her legs numb. She dressed and then stuffed her parents' keepsakes into the saddlebags she'd hidden in the chest. She wouldn't be able to take everything with her this time, the saddlebags too small, but it was better she leave before Axel returned.

First she needed to get past Lars. He sat at the table, his Bible open, his head tipped forward. "Why don't you have a seat, and I'll pour you some coffee, Elizabeth."

She dropped the saddlebags just out of sight in the bedroom before moving toward the stove. "I can pour my own." Halfway across the floor she froze with the realization of what he'd called her. "How long have you known?"

He closed the Bible and looked up. His mouth showed a sad smile. "For sure, I didn't know until you arrived. You've grown a mite since I saw you last, but you look a lot like your Mother...and I already suspected. After the first couple of letters, I remembered why your name had such a familiar ring to it. Danton. After your mother. You probably didn't know this, but I met your mother before her marriage to your father. They were only engaged when your father first started coming to me with his ideas. Three years later I joined him. Just after you were born."

"You knew all along?" Elizabeth sidestepped to the nearest chair and dropped into it. "Then why...?" Why would he bring her out here, let her marry his son and wreak havoc on their lives? Had he guessed she was responsible for the horse and the barn?

"When you wrote of being alone..." Lars stood, took up the kettle and filled a cup. Then set it in front of her. "I contacted some old associates in New York who told me what happened to your family. I felt somewhat responsible. I wanted to make sure you'd be looked after. I felt I owed your parents that much."

Elizabeth clamped a hand over her mouth. Her head throbbed and her empty stomach turned. He owed her father more. Lars Forsberg was still guilty for their ruin, and if he thought he could ever recompense for that...

She pushed away from the table. The legs of the chair squeaked against the floor. "I'm leaving."

Lars stepped around the table, his brows pressing together. "Elizabeth, please wait. Let Axel calm down. Give him a chance to know the truth. I've seen the way he looks at you."

She stumbled back to the bedroom door and fished for the saddlebags. "None of this is about Axel. It never was." Otherwise she might be able to stay. "Please, don't try to stop me."

Lars followed her out into the yard. "Where will you go? And how? Elizabeth, let me help you."

She spun, her anger searing her throat as it released in a scream. "It's all your fault. I don't want your help." A sob choked her, stealing the venom from her voice. "I wanted to ruin you like you ruined us. I wanted to make you miserable...but I only hurt Axel. You made me hurt him. I hate you for bringing me here, for making me feel like I stood a chance at revenge."

***

Lazy cows chewed their cud, chipper birds danced in the trees behind him—a world at odds with the turmoil within Axel. He'd been a fool to marry a complete stranger, but Pa had been certain of her. So much didn't make sense. Why would a woman he'd never met come all the way from New York for the sole purpose of making him miserable?

Blowing out his breath, Axel nudged his horse past the herd and toward the stream. He'd follow it to the border of their land before turning toward home. The only angle that he hadn't considered yet was if the Coopers had hired Eliza—or whatever her name was—to run him and Pa off their land. The notion soured his stomach all the more. She must have laughed at his speech about honesty and his attempts to be a good husband.

Axel followed the stream for almost a mile before he noticed that the current ran a little slower than yesterday. And lower. He encouraged the gelding to a lope until they came to the trail separating Forsberg from Cooper land. Through the trees he could make out horses tied near the rocky bank. The crack of a hammer rang out. Axel slapped his reins against the sides of the saddle and the gelding dug dirt, springing forward into a gallop. He charged up the ridge and around the bend in the stream that shielded a newly constructed dam. Two of the Cooper boys slid another thick plank into place, while a third shoveled mud against the sides.

"What are you doing?"

"Well, well." The eldest straightened. John Cooper wasn't a tall man, but the breadth of his chest and shoulders made up the difference. "You're out and about bright and early this morning."

"Harvey agreed no dams."

"That's Mr. Cooper to you. You ain't your Pa."

Axel swung down from his horse and took a step, his hand instinctively resting over the hilt of his revolver as his temper flared. "Take out the planks."

"Tut tut tut." The youngest, Eli, palmed his own gun. "You think this game only goes one way—that you and your pa can try to burn us out and we'd just stand by?"

"What are you talking about?"

John reached into his pocket and pulled out a tarnished and charred pocket watch, letting it dangle from the chain. "Look familiar? Bet your pa was missing it this morning. You can tell him where to come get it."

Axel turned away so they wouldn't see the emotion he had no hope of masking as everything became clear. "Eliza." That woman. This was all her doing. Heat coursed through him, and his grip tightened on the revolver. When he got home he'd...he'd think of a way to deal with her. And Pa—he was the one who got them into this mess.

Axel spun back to the Coopers. "You—"

Eli stood, his revolver drawn and smoking. Axel's ears rang, slow to register the crack of the gun's discharge. And pain...no, agony. He staggered back and glanced at the small patch of red staining his shirt and the hole in the fabric. Warmth trickled down his side. Black splotches obscured his vision. His knees met the rocky ground. Curse that woman.

***

Thunder echoing off the mountains pulled Elizabeth's focus from the buckle on the cinch. Stitches shifted, perking her ears to the west. "Was that a—"

"Gun shot." Lars stood only paces away. "Could be someone hunting. Or..." He raced back to the cabin.

Axel. He always wore his gun now. And with last night's fire, the Coopers would be a hornet's nest.

Lars grabbed a saddle from just inside the door and ran to where a tall bay stood in the neighboring corral. Elizabeth wouldn't wait. Yanking Stitches' stirrup forward, she untangled the reins from the post and hauled herself into the saddle. A cloud of dust billowed in her wake as her heart skittered out of control. It would be her fault if anything happened to Axel.

She wasn't yet to the stream when Lars passed her on the bay. Up ahead a cluster of men and horses stood on the trail. A shout went up, and the men mounted and whipped their horses back onto Cooper land. One horse remained, a sorrel. Startling, the animal tossed its head and bolted several yards into the meadow. Elizabeth came over a slight rise as the air cleared, the haze of dust settling over the prone form of a man.

Axel!

"Please, God, no."

Elizabeth's heart echoed Lars's cry. Surely God would see Axel was the only faultless one. She and Lars deserved the punishment. Stitches skidded to a halt as Elizabeth yanked on the reins. She half fell to the ground trying to get to Axel faster than her legs could move. Lars beat her to him and rolled him. Blood covered the side of Axel's shirt. He moaned.

Alive.

Elizabeth stood back as Lars ripped open the stained shirt. A small hole oozed scarlet and he pressed his handkerchief over it, then rotated Axel enough to examine the twin hole where the bullet had exited.

"Went straight through," Axel mumbled through gritted teeth. He cast a glance at Elizabeth and glowered. "What are you still doing here? Come to finish me off?"

"I..."

Lars staunched the blood with a handkerchief, and then set Axel's hand over his wound. "Hold this while I get you on the horse. Elizabeth, keep mine steady while I get him up, and then see if the gelding will let you lead him home."

Axel grunted and clamped his eyes closed as his father heaved him to his feet. He didn't try talking again until he was propped up in the saddle. "Is that her real name, or just more lies?"

"We'll discuss this later." Lars swung up behind him and took the reins from Elizabeth's hands, holding her gaze. "You come on back to the cabin. He needs your help."

She gave a nod and backed away as Axel raised his head enough to give her one more glare. "I don't."

They rode away, becoming a blurred haze of color against the green and brown backdrop. Then the tears fell and she with them. To her knees.

Chapter 12

"This is all my fault."

Axel eyed his father as he fastened the ends of the bandage. "Why didn't you tell me?"

"I thought whatever she was going through would work itself out in time. I didn't realize how deeply she blamed me for what her father lost."

At least it explained the sensation of meeting her before. Elizabeth Danton Landvik. The spunky girl with her hair still down and her eyes still big. She'd grown into a handsome woman...and a deadly one. His side pinched as he tried to shift positions. "It wasn't your fault what happened to the Landviks, why should you have bothered with her?"

Pa's lips pressed thin. "Because if I'd stayed there may have been a way to save the company, but I was so weary of keeping it from failing. No matter what I did, every year or so Robert would force us into some scheme that drained the funds. After your mother died, I just couldn't do it anymore, couldn't fight him anymore." He shook his head. "I planned to simply sign everything over to him, the business wasn't worth anything by that time, but Robert Landvik insisted he buy it for my very first investment—the few dollars I'd finally given him to let him know I'd join him." Pa laughed. "A little over four dollars. All the time and years I sunk into him and his fantasies, he figured was worth four dollars."

"Then you should have known better than to try to help his daughter. And to tie me into this mess." Axel wasn't sure who he was angrier with. Elizabeth, for trying to destroy everything they'd built. Pa, for keeping everything secret and marrying him off to an insane and vindictive woman. Or himself, for paying either of them heed and being so distracted by his anger that he'd gotten himself shot.

"Maybe I should have. But she's got nothing, Axel. I still believe that, given the chance, she'll be a good woman. Even a good wife."

"She burned down our barn, Pa."

He sighed. "Yes she did. But what is losing a barn compared to losing both parents?"

Axel let his head drop back into his pillow and covered his face with a hand. His temples throbbed, and the noonday sun did him no service. "I'm exhausted, Pa. Can you make sure she doesn't burn down anything else before we can ship her back where she came from?"

"All right." Pa stood and pulled the blanket over Axel. Mama's quilt. So much for making his marriage like hers and Pa's.

Something beautiful.

Axel closed his eyes and tried not to think about the emptiness of the bed beside him. Strange how after such a short time, that woman had already become a part of his life. What a fool he was.

***

It couldn't be true.

Elizabeth scooted away from the door as footsteps approached. She busied herself at the stove, though not doing anything really, just opening doors to peek inside. As Lars stepped to the table, she reached for a split log. She'd stoke the fire—that was something to do—while trying to work through what Axel's father had told him about hers.

Was he lying?

But why would he lie to his son? If Lars were the type of man she had believed him to be, why show such mercy to her? At the cost of his son?

Lies.

And yet, it could plausibly fit with what she remembered. Her father was angry and blamed Lars for the failing business...because Lars had been the one keeping the business alive, and he'd left. Her father had lost everything. While Lars took his son and made a new life.

She looked at Lars as he lowered into a chair and leaned forward, elbows on the table. His fingers linked, he rested his forehead on them. She'd almost taken everything from him when possibly he'd only been trying to help her.

"I'm sorry." She couldn't seem to put any voice to her words, but he raised his head to glance at her. Even now, his blue eyes held no hate, or even anger. Only sadness and weariness. Elizabeth hurried outside, wiping her clammy palms across her skirts. Everything was her fault and it wasn't over. The Coopers had shot Axel and, according to him, they were building a dam to stop the stream from watering Forsberg land. What else would they do before they felt vindicated? Or would this feud continue to spiral out of control as hers had?

She spun to the fence where the horses waited, still saddled. There hadn't been time to return them to the corrals yet.

Elizabeth glanced back to the cabin, and pressed a hand to her stomach as it did a sudden swoosh. Her pulse sped a clip. The Forsbergs had been hurt enough because of her. She would clean up the mess she started.

Breath hitched in her throat, Elizabeth took long strides to the horses, unfastened Stitches' rein and mounted. One of the other horses gave a whinny as she spurred the little gray mare up the trail and toward the Cooper homestead.

***

The pounding of hooves beating out a departure pulled Axel's eyelids open. The cabin door slammed. Pa shouted something. Then heavy boots trotted back into the cabin and to his room. The door swooshed open. "I have to go after Elizabeth."

Axel winced as he pushed himself up on one of his elbows. "What?"

"She just rode out of here on that gray mare you gave her."

Axel's emotions tugged him from two sides as he lowered himself back to the bed. "She's resourceful enough. She'll find her way back to town."

"I don't think that's where she's going. She packed saddlebags this morning and they're still sitting out in the yard."

"But..." Everything she did left him confused. Maybe it was the blood loss fogging his brain. "I don't understand."

"Coopers." As soon as the word was out of his mouth, Pa hurried away.

"Why, so she can report her success?" Axel hollered after him. He took a slow breath as the throb in his side stabbed. "Wait. Pa?"

His father stuck his head back in the room. "I'm not leaving her to them."

Axel groaned as he laid a hand to his side and rolled into a sitting position on the edge of the bed. His vision darkened momentarily. "Then hitch the wagon."

"Why?"

"Because my head's still spinning too much to stay on a horse. I'm coming with you."

"No, you're not."

"Pa, it's hardly more than a graze. It is not going to kill me. We're going to end this all now, and I'm not going to sit here while you ride into who knows what. I, my Winchester, and my pillow are coming."

Pa didn't look happy about it, but he hitched the wagon. Axel didn't make it out of the cabin with Pa's help before he regretted his decision, but it was too late to turn back. He clenched the gun and gritted his teeth with every rut the wheels jostled over up to the Cooper homestead. As they drove past the barn, Axel got a good view out the back of the wagon of the scorched ground stretching across pasture land. Elizabeth's handiwork, no doubt.

Where was that woman?

The wagon lurched to a halt.

"What are you doing here, Forsberg?" one of the Coopers shouted. Sounded like the eldest. "Come to get your lost filly?"

Axel eased his grip on the rifle as he waited for a wave of nausea to pass. He lifted his shirt just enough to see the red seeping through the bandage. There was nothing for that now. He held his side as he pushed himself up enough to see over the edge of the wagon box. Harvey Cooper stood on the porch of their house, toe to toe with Elizabeth, the boys gathered around. Her eyes widened, then narrowed at seeing Axel, and she spun to fully face him.

"Are you insane? What are you doing out of bed?" She pointed her finger to the trail. "Go home."

"So you can continue plotting my demise?"

Her jaw slackened a little, but Harvey spoke first. "My boys told me about the incident at the dam, and then this woman shows up insisting we end all our differences with you." He looked back to Elizabeth, his voice rising. "But she has yet to tell us who she is."

Axel eased a breath as he sifted to a better position. "She's my wife."

"Your wife?" Harvey shook his head. "She for sure didn't mention that."

"Did she mention she let my horse loose and burned our barn, among other things?" Axel leaned into the side of the wagon and released the Winchester to the floor. Sweat moistened his shirt from the exertion of staying upright.

"Yes, she did. Said something about having a beef against your pa and trying to settle scores."

Axel lowered his hand out of sight so no one would see it tremble. "Then you understand this war she started between us isn't about you. I'll replace the hay you lost and see that she doesn't bother anyone again. But I will also ask you to take that dam down."

The dark-haired middle boy, probably around Elizabeth's age, gave a laugh. "If you can't handle your own wife, maybe you should leave her here. We'll take care of her for you."

Axel shot him a glare. "Eliza, get..." He shifted his gaze to her and hardened his voice.

"Elizabeth, get your horse."

"I was trying to help this time, Axel. After everything I did, I couldn't—"

"You've done enough."

Pa twisted on the seat, his voice low but carrying a warning. "Axel, you—"

"No, Pa. You've done plenty enough, too. She's *my* wife, remember." Pain pierced through his side like a bolt of lightning, its needle-like branches lighting a fire through his whole body. "Elizabeth, on your horse!" As soon as he saw her move to obey, he sank back. Sticky moisture clung to his fingers laid over his bandage, but he no longer had the strength or desire to look. He should have stayed home. "Do we have a deal, Harvey?"

"Sure," the man grumbled. "We'll call it even for now. Just keep that filly of yours off our land."

Axel closed his eyes. Now to figure out what to do with his bride. Though she deserved to be left stranded at Bumble Bee, he'd gladly buy her a ticket to wherever she wanted...just to be rid of her. He'd rather not admit it, even to himself, but more than just the hole in his side needed time to heal.

***

Elizabeth held her hands only inches from the stove, craving the heat though the day was by no means chill. Boots echoed against the floor behind her, but she didn't want to look at him yet. "Is Axel...is he going to be all right?"

"He'll be fine," Lars answered as he neared. Thankfully he stopped at the far end of the table. "He lost more blood, but he should heal as long as he gives himself some time."

Breathing came easier now. She hugged herself with her warm hands. "I should leave."

"Should you?"

She choked on a laugh and turned. "Surely you don't want me here any longer. After everything I did. I'm not blinded anymore to think that you owed my father anything. And even if you did, surely nothing compared to what I have put Axel through." She lowered her gaze to the floor, no longer able to meet his steady one. "I heard what you told Axel about my father. That was the truth, wasn't it?"

"Yes."

Not that Elizabeth required his answer. Deep down she already knew. The need to blame someone had dissipated in the heat of her shame. She slipped her hand into the pocket of her apron and pinched the ribbon between her fingers, drawing out the silken pouch. She extended it over the table and set it in Lars's palm. "These are yours."

The ridges of his brow deepened as he pulled it open and looked inside. "How did you...?"

"I thought because the box was locked it must be where you kept your money—money I thought you'd cheated my father out of. I needed it if I was to leave this place so I...broke in."

"I kept that box locked for my own sanity. Axel keeps the key." Lars drew out the ring, slipping it on to the very tip of one finger. "This has been in our family for a couple of generations now. Camilla wore it. And my mother." His mouth formed a sad smile. "It should be yours. Axel was planning to give it to you. When the time was right."

"The time never would have been right." Elizabeth blinked back the burn of tears. She'd already cried more in the past twenty-four hours than the previous nine years, and she wasn't finished, but not right now. Axel probably slept, and for his sake she didn't want to be here when he awoke.

"It's still early enough," she said. "If I borrow Stitches, I should reach Bumble Bee before dark. I'll leave her there for you."

Lars's gaze remained heavy on her as she walked to the door and collected the saddlebags with her belongings. "And how will you get home?"

The question haunted her, but she couldn't possibly ask for money. "I'll find a way." Her voice carried much more confidence than she felt. She reached for the door latch.

"Elizabeth, you're not going anywhere tonight. Come back to the table and sit down. I'll fix some supper, and later I'll make up a bed for myself out here."

She pressed her eyes closed against a flood and hugged the saddlebags. "Why?" Why would he still want to help her when she should be run off, or hauled away by the nearest US marshal? Why such mercy?

But there it was—forgiveness. Love, despite everything she had done. And if Lars could show her such...perhaps God would, as well.

Chapter 13

Axel gazed out the window at the same tiny patch of blue sky he'd been staring at for the past three days. Flat on his back. He changed his view to the door but a kink already burned in his neck. The rumble of voices in the main room only made his temper flare. They probably sat at the table talking about the past, about Elizabeth's parents, or what she'd done with herself since their deaths. Or maybe they read from the Bible about hope and forgiveness...again.

Either way, he didn't want to hear it.

Unfortunately, with all these hours left to himself, he couldn't help searching his memory for ones of her as a child, her hair curled, and her eyes bright. Ribbons and bows. Youthful innocence as she tried to catch his eye. Five years her senior, he hadn't considered her flirtations, but those years had shrunk significantly in the past nine. It was strange to now see her as a grown woman and to recognize her.

Even stranger how empty his room and his bed felt without her beside him.

Until he remembered the pile of charred debris not fifty paces from the cabin.

Pa's footsteps preceded a knock.

"What?"

He entered and closed the door. "We should talk."

Axel was hardly in the mood, but that mood wasn't likely to change any time soon. "Fine. What do you want to say?"

Pulling up a chair, Pa seated himself and leaned his elbows on his knees. "Elizabeth has been asking about a ride down to Bumble Bee. She doesn't want to ask, but we should pay her fare—at least enough for the stage to Phoenix."

"Supplies for rebuilding the barn will make cash tight enough." Axel blew out his breath. The action made him wince. "Fine, we can manage that much. Send her all the way back to New York if that's what she wants."

"What do you want?"

Axel pushed up higher, stuffing another pillow behind him. "Now you're asking me?"

"I didn't force you to marry her. In the end it was your choice."

"After she was already on her way. Not to

mention, you led me to believe she was everything she portrayed in those letters. It was all a lie. It wasn't a marriage. How could it have—how could it ever be?"

Pa's arms folded across his chest, a pose Axel would have gladly taken if it didn't hurt so badly. "Son, she's still your wife. And I believe she has come to care for you."

Axel forced a laugh—again, not a wise move. "In the two—three weeks she's been here? Most of which time she used me to get revenge at you." He shook his head and glanced back to the window. "But of course, why should I be upset with her? *You* started all this by using me to bring her here. I don't want to talk about it anymore. You'll have to be content to let me live my own life. And I plan to live it alone up here, because right now, that's what *I* want." Leaning his head back he balled his fist and pressed his thumb into the sore spot between his eyes. "I'll take her down to Bumble Bee myself as soon as I've healed enough."

Standing, Pa nodded and reached into his shirt pocket. "Why don't we give it a week or so, then—see if you change your mind." He withdrew Mama's ring and placed it on the bed beside Axel before turning to go.

Axel locked his jaw as he took up the priceless heirloom, beautiful and unique like the quilt, and meant for his marriage—his wife. "I'm not changing my mind, Pa." There was no way.

***

Elizabeth rubbed the thin white blaze on Stitches' face. "Good bye, girl. I'll miss you." And so much about this place. The towering mountains, the way the sun rose over them, the cattle's low bellows, and everything about the horses. She couldn't return to New York after experiencing the freedom and scope of this place—no buildings to block the sun's splendor as it slipped below the horizon. Hopefully she'd be able to make a life for herself in Phoenix. If not, she'd try California.

"We're about ready here," Lars called.

Axel stood beside him fussing with the straps across the horses' backs. Anything to avoid her. His father had hitched the wagon before loading the small chest with her things into the back.

Oh, Axel. She would miss him the most.

She turned to Stitches and patted her forehead. They'd told Elizabeth she could keep the little mare, but as much as she would have loved to, she would never feel right about that after everything she'd done.

One farewell said, a ride down the mountains, and two more remained. She would have preferred to say goodbye to Axel here—though he'd gotten so good at not acknowledging her presence, he might not return it—but for reasons that eluded her, he insisted he would be the one to deliver her to the stagecoach. Probably just wanted to make sure she left.

Fortifying herself with a breath, Elizabeth strode to the wagon and Lars. He wrapped her in an embrace. "Write to us now and again and let us know how you get on."

A nod was all she could supply. She pressed a kiss to his cheek. Over the last two weeks, all her notions of this man had been flipped on their heads. His kindness, his forgiveness, and all that gentle wisdom he'd fed her soul now gave new understanding.

"I will," she said after a moment. "Thank you."

Lars boosted her onto the wagon seat beside Axel. The older man looked to his son. "I still think you're a fool for thinking you can handle this rig again so soon. You're going to do yourself damage if you're not careful."

"I'll be careful." Axel followed his terse growl with the slap of leather lines against horse flesh. "Giddy-up."

Lars stepped out of the way, face grim. Elizabeth waved before settling into her seat and focusing forward. She could see Axel's granite expression out of the corner of her eye, looking as stoic as an executioner following through with a sentence. The verdict had been given, and she could not refute it. Undeniable and horribly guilty.

The next few hours passed in slow motion, not a word said between them, and yet the twig of a town appeared ahead of them all too soon. The stagecoach waited in the same place she'd seen it a month earlier. An absent driver meant he probably hurried with his dinner so they could be on their way. Elizabeth's ribs constricted her breath better than any corset. Panic surged through her as she looked to Axel. Once she got on that stage, she would never see him again. If there was only a way to freeze time until she could figure a way to turn it back—or convince him to forgive her.

"Axel?"

He glanced at her, his lips pressed thin. To think of the times they had pressed gently to her hair as his palm warmed her shoulder. Or the couple of times they had found her mouth and silently spoken of his desire for her. He might have grown to love her if she'd let him.

"I know I said it already, and you have little

reason to believe me, but I am sorry. For everything." Except for loosing herself in his arms that one morning. If only there were a way to go back.

As usual, he answered with silence, the muscles in his jaw working. He pulled the wagon to a halt across the street from the station.

"You're a good man, Axel Forsberg. Thank you for being the husband any girl would be lucky...blessed...to have for her own. Maybe someday..." Hope fled her. Elizabeth pivoted away and jumped down from the wagon seat, not sure what she would have said. There was no someday. She needed to get herself on that stagecoach and not look back.

Vision swimming, she hastened across the street. Then slid to a halt as the stage driver, Sam, burst through the station door. He looked from her to Axel and raised his hand in a wave, before motioning behind him. "I just left a note to be given to you next time you came into town. It's in there with your shipment of nails and hinges. Sent word to St. Louis for you and heard back from them before I left Phoenix Wednesday. They said they'd freight out that piano you wanted, so I went ahead and sent the money you gave me for it. So there you are. Your piano is on its way."

Elizabeth rotated to Axel, her heart both skipping a beat and plunging to her boots in the same instant. "A piano?"

He made a slight nod as he met her gaze. The blue in his eyes glistened and his expression lost some of its severity. "Yep."

"How were you going to get a piano up to the ranch?"

"Same way we hauled up the stove. I figured a piano would be lighter."

"But..." He was going to do that for her? Why? "When?"

He swallowed. "After we talked and you said you didn't want to leave. That night you rode to the Coopers and set fire to their hay."

She covered her mouth with the tips of her fingers, but it could only hide the tremble of her chin, not the welling in her eyes. Her mind told her to turn away from him, to not let him see what he did to her, but she couldn't remove her gaze from him, even as it hazed.

"Did you mean what you said that day?" He took a step forward. "Or was it more lies. Did you want to stay?"

"I did."

Another step. "And now?"

"I do."

Three more steps and Axel's strong hands braced her shoulders. "Tell me truthfully,

Elizabeth. Don't even color the truth."

She held his gaze as it penetrated her. "I never want to leave you. Or hurt you again. Ever."

***

Axel didn't budge, or hardly blink. He wanted so much to believe her, to forgive her, but trust seemed too far out of reach. Much too far. He had no choice but to let her go. To put her on that stagecoach.

Yet so much hope shone in those pretty eyes of hers. And tears tumbled down her cheeks.

She probably just wanted to stay because she had nowhere else to go. Using her womanly wiles to weaken his resolve.

"It would never work." He dropped his hands to his sides. "You don't belong here."

"Of course, I don't." Her voice gave a squeak as she spun away and stepped to the door of the station. She gripped the latch. "That is, I didn't." Slowly, Elizabeth rotated back to him, her hand wiping across her cheeks as she blinked her eyes dry. "I was angry, and a perfect mess inside. I should never have come. But I don't regret it."

He opened his mouth, but she held up her

hand.

"I regret everything I did—the lies, the open gate, the fires." She shook her head. "But I can't regret coming here. I can't regret finding God again. The feeling being wanted and cherished. Or being a part of a family." She filled her lungs as she held his gaze. "I don't regret falling in love with you."

Elizabeth turned and pushed into the station office, leaving Axel to stare after her, and Sam to chuckle.

"Sounds like your marriage has been a right interesting one thus far," the stage driver said, striding past. "Reckon it can only get better from here on out."

Axel glanced to the man as he moved to the stagecoach. The horses looked fresh. Which meant there wasn't much time to get a ticket bought and load Elizabeth and her luggage. But instead Axel stood in place, mulling over what life with that woman might be like from *here on out*. It wasn't as though he had another barn to burn. And he'd already been shot. Couldn't get much worse. One thing was for sure, though. After the past month, life would be rather dull without Elizabeth, and his bed was already mighty empty.

He glanced to the heavens. As much as he'd tried to hide behind his anger, Axel couldn't deny the change the last couple weeks had wrought in Elizabeth. She wasn't the same woman who had stepped off of that stage...but much more like the one he had been expecting to.

Axel charged through the station door. And right into Elizabeth. She hadn't gone very far.

"Swear to me you're telling the truth, woman," he said bracing her arms.

Her eyes widened with such hope, he couldn't help himself. He leaned down and pressed his mouth to hers. She stiffened momentarily before melting against him, her hands slipping around him, her fingers finding the hair at the nape of his neck. The way her lips moved against his sent a fire right through him.

Finally, he relaxed his hold enough to look down into the large brown eyes that had been his bane.

"What do you think?" she asked slightly out of breath.

"I think the pastor's long gone from town."

Her brow crinkled. "Why would we—?"

"Because I don't know what the laws in Arizona Territory are for marrying under an assumed name, and I'm not taking any chances." Axel's wound pinched with the reminder that he was a glutton for punishment if he kept her, but there was nothing for that now. Besides, Mama would roll over in her grave if he didn't set things right. "I'm going to marry Elizabeth Landvik right and proper." He led her outside and toward the cavalry station. "I have an idea."

It wasn't long before he'd tracked down Captain Gray and stood Elizabeth before him as a simple ceremony was performed. Axel's fingers intertwined with hers as the captain concluded his words. He gave Axel a smile. "Mr. Forsberg, you may kiss your bride."

Axel turned Elizabeth to him. Her full lips beckoned, and he planned to start this marriage right.

Then they'd make it something beautiful.

Author's Note

I hope you enjoyed this story. If you did, please join me on some future adventures. Here are a couple coming your way!

Prism Book Group / Inspired Publishing
    Her Blue-eyed Brave (2017)

Pelican Book Group / White Rose Publishing
    Hearts at War series:
        The Scarlet Coat (Jan 27, 2017)
        The Patriot and the Loyalist (2017)

To keep informed, pop by my website, www.angelakcouch.com, and sign up for my newsletter or follow me on Facebook or Twitter.

Acknowledgements

Thank you to all those who have helped bring this story come to life! To my amazing critique partners who have put so much time into pouring over each sentence with me. To my enthusiastic beta readers. Rachel Pedersen, my editor. Jessica Sprong, my *amazing* cover artist who was able to make my vision a reality. And a huge "thank you" to all my encouraging friends and family...especially my very patient husband!

Most of all, I thank the Lord for blessing me with this story to tell.

Made in the USA
Middletown, DE
01 February 2017